NEON–COLORED SPIDER WEBS

TAD TROILO

Neon-colored Spider Webs

Set in Miller Text Roman
Printed in the United States of America
First edition, 2011

Markham Road Press
markhamroadpress@me.com

ISBN–13: 978-1461180777
ISBN–10: 1461180775

NEON-COLORED SPIDER WEBS

Stewart lost the baseball before he even got it to school. This was bad.

The baseball, signed by none other than Moe Berg, had been lent to him by his grandfather, Big Pops, for the express purpose of making Stewart cool. It would be hard to be cool with no baseball to show off. And it would be hard to explain to Big Pops just exactly how he had lost the ball before showing it to a single student at West Plain High.

Actually, Big Pops probably wouldn't care about *how* he lost it. He'd care most about the *lost* part.

He loved that baseball. He kept it on display on top of the TV set in the living room.

"Like to keep my eye on that ball," Big Pops would say now and then, for no apparent reason, which wasn't weird for him at all. "That ball makes money."

"How?" Stewart asked him one day when it dawned on him that's what Big Pops wanted him to ask.

"Whaaale," Big Pops answered. He was saying 'well,' but it really didn't sound like 'well.' It didn't quite sound like 'whale' either. But that's how he pronounced it every time he said it, and he said it a lot. It was usually followed by a proclamation that sounded like it made sense, but really didn't. "A man's got to step up the plate and deliver, and that ball proves that fact for certain."

Like that.

Neither the way he pronounced 'well,' nor the cryptic words that followed were weird for Big Pops at all.

What *was* weird for Big Pops was that he had lent the ball to Stewart.

"Don't you think you'd like to be cool?" he asked that morning, sitting in his recliner, eating his pork roll and toast breakfast on the TV tray in front of him.

Even though he lived with him now, Stewart didn't know his grandfather very well. This was mostly due to the fact that Big Pops had spent seven years in prison.

That's right. Prison.

His parents never told Stewart what his grandfather went to prison for. All he knew was every year on his grandfather's birthday, Stewart's mom and dad would cart him off to visit Big Pops.

It's hard to get to know someone while visiting them in prison. The visits were short, held in a large, loud room with dozens of tables filled with other families visiting other inmates while angry guards patrolled the aisles.

It was scary.

And so, to Stewart, Big Pops became scary too.

When he got out of prison, Big Pops came to visit once. Stewart hid in his room.

So even after Stewart moved in with his grandfather, there was distance between them.

Stewart was bright enough to know that this distance was made greater by the fact that Big Pops was a little scared of Stewart. You wouldn't think Big Pops would be afraid of anything. He was a tall man, slim and strong, with white hair so short you might not notice it. He looked a lot like Stewart's father, but he smiled less.

Despite his tough look, Stewart was sure his grandfather was in fact a little afraid of him. It had been a long time since he had taken care of a kid. He didn't really know what to do with his grandson. Big Pops never asked Stewart what he was up to or interested in. He never asked about homework, or checked to see if he was making friends at his new school.

And, in turn, Stewart was still too scared of Big Pops to offer up this information himself.

They both remained wary of the situation, and of each other, so when Big Pops presumed to know that Stewart would want to bring a baseball to school to be cool, it was, as mentioned, weird.

Big Pops pointed a pork roll laden fork at the TV, which was showing the morning news.

"Take the ball," he said. "Show it off a little."

He knew why his grandfather assumed correctly that Stewart wasn't cool. Stewart was on the short side of things, a little chunky and wore big glasses on his small face that were often partially covered by the bangs of his completely unremarkable light brown hair. He moved through the halls of his school with the timidness of the new student coupled with the awkwardness of the nonathletic. Stewart was also impossibly bright and couldn't help but be identified as a brain by other students.

While much has certainly changed since Big Pops went to high school, Stewart was sure these time-honored classic signs of 'not cool' had remained the same.

Stewart shrugged his shoulders as he ate his pork roll on a matching TV tray, sitting on the couch. He didn't know what to say, so he just pushed his glasses up his nose and shrugged his shoulders.

He didn't really want to take the ball to school. There were a lot or things that Stewart wanted just then, but being cool wasn't one of them.

"You sure?" Stewart asked, not wanting to brush off Big Pops' efforts.

"Oh yeah," Big Pops said, smiling. "I'm sure."

Stewart shrugged again, cleared, his plate and put the ball in his backpack.

Then, while leaning his head against the window of the bus thinking about Band-Aids and bags of rice, he heard a soft thud and knew with an odd certainty that the ball had fallen out of his unzipped backpack onto the floor of the bus. He knelt down on the floor and looked toward the front of the bus. He saw the ball rolling through the forest of legs hanging over the seats. It serpentined its way toward the front of the bus as it decelerated.

A lesser mind might have been confused by this. The bus slowing, yet the ball rolling forward. Stewart didn't think twice about the physics of this.

He did have to think twice about whose hand reached down into the leg forest to snatch up the baseball. In fact he had to think about it a few times.

Often, while thinking, Stewart engaged parts of his body in conversation. This is what that conversation sounded like:

STEWART: I can see a hand grabbing the ball, but I can't see it clearly. Eyes, focus.

EYES: We're trying.

STEWART: Can you try harder?

EYES: We are.

BRAIN: They can't see that far. They have astigmatism.

STEWART: They have to. We have to see that hand.

BRAIN: And even if they see that hand, what good will that do us?

STEWART: If we can see the hand, we'll know who has the baseball.

BRAIN: Oh really? You are going to recognize a kid on a bus based on his hand?

STEWART: Oh.

BRAIN: You know what every kid's hands look like?

STEWART: Okay—

BRAIN: You've memorized the hands of all the kids on this bus?

STEWART: OKAY.

BRAIN: We need to think of a different way to solve this problem.

STEWART: Yes, we do.

BRAIN: I've thought of different way to solve this problem.

STEWART: What?

BRAIN: Count.

STEWART: Count what?

BRAIN: Count legs.

STEWART: Oh. Good idea.

BRAIN: I know. Eyes—

EYES: We're on it.

BRAIN: Based on four legs per seat, we should be able to calculate what seat that hand is coming from. Then, cross-referenced with our memory of who is sitting where, we will be able to conclude who has the baseball.

EYES: We see twenty-two legs between us and the hand.

STEWART: That's five and a half seats. There can't be a half of a seat.

BRAIN: Of course not. One seat only has two legs.

STEWART: So someone is sitting alone.

EYES: That's the seat with the hand.

BRAIN: So that person has the ball.

STEWART: Who is sitting alone, six seats in front of us?

BRAIN: Cunningham.

The fact that this conversation took less than half a second did not lessen the severity of the terror Stewart felt upon reaching its conclusion.

He slowly picked himself up off the floor and sat back in his seat. Six seats ahead of him, he saw Cunningham plop the baseball into his backpack with his left hand while punching a boy named Steven in the back of the head.

Cunningham was the second biggest bully at West Plain High. He stood a towering six feet, six inches tall, and weighed in around two hundred and seventy-five pounds. One reason he was sitting alone on the bus was the simple fact that no one else could fit on the seat with him. Another reason was he enjoyed his personal space.

Cunningham's crew cut hair made no effort to hide his immense, block-like head. His shirt tried to hide his giant arms but failed. Speaking of failing, he had been held back in the grades of high school seven times. He rode the bus because he also failed his driving test seven times.

Stewart knew at once that he would need a good plan to recover the baseball.

Stewart liked plans. He deeply enjoyed their orderly and organized nature and the satisfaction of completing one step by step. It is safe to say plans were one of Stewart's favorite things and he made a lot of them.

So he immediately formulated several plans to recover the baseball. These first plans were simple and obvious, like sneaking the ball out of Cunningham's backpack while the bully was busy punching someone on the bus or the straightforward asking Cunningham for the ball back.

Stewart felt these plans would end in failure, bodily harm to him, or more likely both, so he rejected them all.

He would need a better plan.

Which was fine. He was just getting warmed up. He relished the challenge.

But first, he would need to read the table.

That was a poker term.

The bus pulled up in front of West Plain High. All the kids stood up, gathered their things and waited. After Cunningham stepped into the aisle and sauntered off the bus, the other kids poured out behind him.

This, of course, was the usual routine. And usually, the kids pouring out behind the sauntering Cunningham would in turn be followed by a toddling Stewart.

But this was not a usual day. Stewart had to read the table.

As soon as Cunningham put one foot in the aisle, Stewart thrust himself out of his seat in an effort to beat the other kids and stay close behind Cunningham.

Stewart was pretty small and very new at West Plain High, and therefore mostly invisible. Before he could take three steps, all the kids behind him pushed their way in front of him and just like that, he was back into his usual position.

When he finally got off the bus Stewart locked his eyes on the backpack on Cunningham's massive back, its straps stretched and straining. The giant strolled leisurely toward the entrance of the school as the rest of the student body swarmed around him, careful not to get to close, or God forbid, to touch him.

In order to read the table, Stewart would have to observe Cunningham. He would have to learn his schedule, his habits, his tendencies. With this information, he was confident he could create a plan that would lead to the recovery of the baseball.

Being mostly invisible made it easy for Stewart to follow Cunningham unnoticed into the school and down the main hall. Kids were hustling here and there, heading to their lockers to get their books, running to find a teacher or a friend. Cunningham calmly, slowly, deliberately kept walking down the center of the wide main aisle, like a moving island in a turbulent sea—a sea that never once would break on the fleshy shores of the island for fear of getting punched.

Since the kids had no reason to fear Stewart, they had no incentive not to bump, jostle or ram into him. So they did. A lot.

But that is not to suggest they noticed him when they did, because they didn't. He remained mostly invisible.

It was like the students were hitting an obscured obstacle when they struck Stewart. They would wordlessly spin off in another direction, annoyed that something unseen had blocked their path.

So his progress down the hall was less graceful than his target.

Things improved for him as the first bell rang telling the sea of students that they had precisely three minutes to get to their first period class. Kids headed down the smaller halls that lead to the various wings of the school.

Then things got really easy when Cunningham turned down the music wing. In fact, suddenly, there were only two people in the hall: Stewart and the second biggest bully at West Plain High.

Stewart knew the equation that governed Student Invisibility:

Student Invisibility (%) = 100 {IP × $\sqrt[3]{(K \div H)}$}

IP = Invisibility Potential (Stewart's was a very high .92)
K = Number of kids in hallway
H= Maximum capacity of hallway

As you can see, the more kids around, the more invisible a student became. Just as obvious is the fact that the fewer kids the more *visible* a student became.

Which was a problem.

It took Stewart less than one tenth of one second to perform the necessary calculations regarding his current Student Invisibility and to conclude it was unacceptably low. At this moment, he was dangerously visible.

It took Cunningham three seconds to hear Stewart's footsteps behind him.

Stewart froze.

Cunningham turned.

Stewart continued to freeze.

Cunningham looked toward Stewart, who as we know, was now clearly visible.

Stewart entertained the notion that really, there was nothing to worry about. They were just two fellow students in the hallway of West Plain High. Schoolmates. Comrades. Preparing for yet another day's grind in the classrooms. That it appeared that one (Stewart), was following the other (Cunningham) should be of no consequence.

But among other things, Stewart was a realist. So as quickly as he had these thoughts he dismissed them. Historically speaking, situations like this—being alone in a hall with a bully—did not end well. So even before Cunningham spoke, he knew he was in trouble.

"What do you want?" the hulk grunted in a deep, methodical voice.

Stewart took approximately 1.3 seconds to review fourteen different responses, reject them all, choosing instead a quickly devised fifteenth.

"Me?"

"You're the only one here."

"No I'm not," Stewart pointed out. "There's you."

"Me?"

"Exactly," Stewart offered, pleased by the symmetry of the conversation.

Cunningham blinked a few times, then refocused on Stewart.

"What do you want?" he said, louder this time.

Stewart recognized the familiar pattern. Bully asks an open ended question. Victim offers explanation. Bully, not satisfied, asks question again. Bloodshed follows.

Giving in to the inevitable, Stewart remained silent, shrugging his shoulders and preparing to run.

"You want in?" Cunningham said, nodding his head toward a door marked 'Xylophone Practice Room.'

There were four surprising things about that question:

West Plain High owned a xylophone.
West Plain High thought highly enough of the xylophone to dedicate a practice room to the instrument.
Cunningham was a xylophone player.

*Cunningham was trying to engage him in a conversa-
tion. In fact, he seemed to be inviting him in to
practice the xylophone.*

This was uncharted territory for Stewart. He had never engaged in conversation with a bully before. He also had never played the xylophone.

He allowed himself two full seconds to analyze the situation before opening his mouth to speak.

He was going to say 'sure,' but the principal of West Plain High stopped him by grabbing Stewart's collar from behind and dragging him down the hall to his office.

Because he was relatively new to West Plain High, the principal had Stewart fill out a Student Information Form on a clip board. The principal leaned back in his fabric chair behind his desk, staring at Stewart through squinted eyes, his bushy mustache, bunched up over his pursed lips.

Stewart, who could multi-task with the best of them, asked a few questions as he filled in the form.

"What are the charges?" he asked.

"Roaming the halls," The principal answered.

"Is it possible I was on my way to class?" Stewart wondered.

"No."

"Why not?"

"You don't have a class in the music wing first period."

"How did you know that when you apprehended me?" Stewart said, hazarding a confident glance at the principal.

"No one has a class in the music wing first period."

Huh.

Stewart realized the principal had the upper hand.

"Can I see an attorney?" he asked returning to his form.

"No."

Which was fine with Stewart. He was just stalling.

"What about Cunningham?" he asked.

"You want to see Cunningham?"

"Does he have a class in the music wing first period?"

"I said no one has a class in the music wing first period."

"Except Cunningham?"

"Including Cunningham."

"Then why wasn't he apprehended as well?" Stewart asked in a tone that he thought nicely suggested 'checkmate.'

The principal rocked slowly forward in his reclining chair. The chair let out a piercing squeak until finally the principal's elbows were on his desk. He leaned his bald head down to Stewart's level and paused for effect before speaking.

"Two cars are speeding down the highway," he started, his hands leaping from the desk suddenly to illustrate his story. "One is red, one is blue. They're both going one hundred miles an hour. A police car is parked on the side of the road." He snapped his head to the right, apparently spotting the police car. "Wham! He tracks him with his speed radar gun. The police car pulls out onto the highway and runs into pursuit."

Stewart was pretty sure that last sentence was grammatically incorrect.

"There are two cars speeding," the principal continued. "But only one police car. What should he do?"

The principal raised his eyebrows at him and Stewart realized the question wasn't rhetorical.

"He should call for backup," Stewart said.

"Backup is not available," the principal countered.

"Why not?"

"Backup is busy."

"The whole police force is busy?"

"That's right. There is an emergency across town."

"Why isn't this police car at the emergency?" Stewart asked.

"Because he's chasing the blue and red cars."

"But—"

"Which car should he pull over?" the principal snapped. "That's the question we are working on here."

"Oh."

"Well?"

"The red car," Stewart said confidently. This was a 'bluff.' That also is a poker term.

"Why not the blue car?"

"Okay. The blue car."

"Why not the red car?" the principal said with his own version of the 'checkmate' tone.

"I see," Stewart said, and of course he did now.

"Do you?"

"But I think the police man could really just take both kids to the office because they aren't really cars speeding down the highway."

"That is not the point," the principal said sharply. "The point is, he pulls over the red car. And the red car driver might say, 'What about the blue car?' And the police man might say, 'Well, what about it? Doesn't matter that the blue car was speeding. You, red car, were speeding too.'"

Stewart nodded, but his nod obviously offended the principal somehow because he continued his sharp lecture.

"How do you know the blue car didn't have some place to be? Huh? How do you know what the blue car was really doing, speeding down the highway? You don't. So I suggest to you, you worry about your own red car, young man."

With that, the principal reached over his desk and snatched Stewart's Student Information Form off the clipboard, settled back into his squeaking chair and scanned it. Stewart could tell by the twitching of the principal's mustache that he didn't believe what he was reading.

But every word of it was true.

A day at school typically had two opposite but equally unpleasant effects on Stewart.

The first effect was boredom. Stewart was a bright kid. He learned things quickly, read things fast and remembered everything. You might think those attributes would make him an excellent student. But Stewart being Stewart never got noticed by teachers as an academic overachiever. They didn't seem to notice that he had answers in the fall to questions that wouldn't be asked until the spring.

So he would get bored with the lessons, sometimes before they even began.

The second effect was terror. While teachers didn't seem to notice Stewart's brainy abilities, other kids sure did. And Stewart being Stewart, this would make him a target for bullies.

You might be wondering what 'Stewart being Stewart' means.

Here is an example:

In his last school, when his class studied atomic particles, Stewart quickly grew tired of *studying* protons, electrons and neutrons and instead decided to *become* one.

He chose the electron. This, the most elusive of the three, would allow him to be there while not being there, a trick he tried out in the cafeteria that day at lunch by sitting down on the varsity football linebacker.

That's right. On.

He simply walked up to the table filled with football players, shimmed his way between the linebacker and the table and sat on his lap.

Here is a transcript of the ensuing conversation:

LINEBACKER: What are you doing?

STEWART: Me?

LINEBACKER: Get off my lap.

STEWART: No need.

LINEBACKER: Why not?

STEWART: I'm an electron.

LINEBACKER: A what?

STEWART: An electron.

LINEBACKER: So?

STEWART: So my exact location is unknowable.

LINEBACKER: GET OFF MY LAP!

STEWART: I might be off it already.

LINEBACKER: Good.

STEWART: I might be three seats over.

LINEBACKER: I'm gonna knock you through the window if you don't get off my lap.

STEWART: I might be through the window already.

LINEBACKER: Huh?

STEWART: Or I might be in the library—

LINEBACKER: I'm counting to three.

STEWART: —or the playground.

LINEBACKER: One.

STEWART: But you can predict my whereabouts—

LINEBACKER: Two.

STEWART: —by relating me to the closest proton.

LINEBACKER: Three.

The rest of the transcript is filled with the sound of a football player beating up a shorter than average, smarter than average kid with brown hair and glasses that would soon be broken.

It's not that Stewart meant to cause trouble.

It's not that he wanted to get beaten up.

It's not that he was trying to do anything except have what he thought was a little fun at school.

School became a constant struggle with boredom, which he would fend off with fun that might well get him beaten up, a concern which induced terror. But Stewart was smart enough to know that he was not the first kid to have these issues at school. He reasoned that many—perhaps even most—of those kids survived their educational experiences, so chances are, he would too.

And anyway, at the end of every school day he always had home to come home to.

But this year, things were different.

Now he had Big Pops' house to come home to.

Which wasn't home. It was a house he lived in now, with a grandfather he hardly knew on account of the time he spent in prison.

And today was really different.

Now he had Big Pops' house to come home to without Big Pops' baseball signed by none other than Moe Berg.

On the bus ride home he spent approximately twenty-seven seconds trying to formulate a plan for explaining this to Big Pops.

He failed.

He then vowed to focus on getting the ball back, and reviewed all the information he gathered while reading the table.

This is what he knew:

Cunningham had the ball in his backpack.
Cunningham played the xylophone.
*The principal equated Cunningham to a blue car. The
    meaning of this was unclear.*
*Though he had been on the lookout for him, Stewart
    hadn't seen Cunningham the rest of the day. He
    didn't see him in the halls between classes, or in the
    cafeteria for lunch. He only saw the second biggest
    bully at West Plain High on the bus to and from
    school and in the music wing hallway. The mean-
    ing of this was also unclear.*

Stewart went over the short list more than twenty times in four seconds.

He then spent one hundred and twenty seconds watching the back of Cunningham's head. The second biggest bully at West Plain High was swatting at any kid who happened to get inside the radius of arms. Stewart could just barely see the top of the backpack containing the baseball sitting on Cunningham's lap.

He then spent the remaining one thousand one hundred and forty-six seconds of the bus ride being sad.

The principal had given Stewart a written warning slip that had to be signed by Big Pops. Stewart reasoned, with a high degree of certainty, that upon presenting the written warning slip to Big Pops, a conversation would ensue regarding the nature of the infraction, the circumstances surrounding the infraction and the consequences of the infraction. During this conversation he would inevitably have to tell Big Pops about the lost baseball.

As they enjoyed their normal Monday dinner of pizza and celery, Stewart showed Big Pops the slip.

"This is from the principal," Stewart said, his voice cracking from both the hot peppers on the pizza and his nerves. "You have to sign it."

"Huh," Big Pops said, holding the slip close to his eyes.

"Should I get your glasses?" Stewart asked.

"For what?"

"So you can read it."

"I don't need to read it," Big Pops told him. "I just need to sign it."

"Oh."

Stewart handed him a pen.

"Where do I sign it?" Big Pops asked.

"Right where it says 'Big Pops.'"

"How come it says that?" Big Pops asked while signing.

"Because that's where you sign," Stewart answered.

"How come they know my name?"

"Because I told them," Stewart answered, wondering how the principal had become 'them' in this conversation.

"You did?"

"I did."

"You think that was smart?"

"Sure."

"What else did you tell them?" Big Pops asked.

For the second time that day, Stewart bluffed.

"Nothing."

Stewart knew that to be successful while bluffing, one had to act normally, control your breathing, look calm, so he tried to do all those things.

Big Pops squinted at Stewart carefully.

"Whaaale," Big Pops said, putting down the signed slip and getting up from the table. "Sometimes the easy stuff is tougher than the tough stuff, isn't it Stewart?"

"Um," Stewart said. "I guess so."

"Eat your celery."

"I did."

"Then eat mine too," Big Pops said, pushing away his TV tray and grabbing his laptop computer.

As Stewart ate Big Pops' celery, Big Pops leaned back in his recliner, turned on the TV and started up his computer.

"Time to make the rent," Big Pops shouted.

Stewart knew Big Pops would spend the rest of the night with his computer in front of the TV playing online poker for money.

He never even asked about the baseball.

Until Tuesday morning.

"Did it make you cool?" Big Pops asked as he saw Stewart to the door.

"What?" Stewart stalled.

"The baseball," Big Pops asked. "Did it make you cool?"

"Oh sure," Stewart said, putting on his backpack. He was getting a a lot of practice bluffing.

"Good, good," Big Pops said. "You got your money for lunch?"

"*Have*," Stewart said, correcting his grandfather.

"Huh?"

"Do I *have* my money for lunch."

"How would I know?" Big Pops said. "That's what I asked you."

"I have my money," Stewart said.

Stewart had one foot out the door, hoping that was the end of the chit-chat for the morning.

But it wasn't.

"Wait!" Big Pops shouted. Stewart turned around and Big Pops shoved a paper at him. "You forgot this thing for them."

Stewart grabbed the written warning slip, but Big Pops didn't let go.

"Where is it, anyway?" Big Pops asked.

"Where is what?"

"The baseball."

"Oh," Stewart said. "In my locker. Thought I'd like to be cool another day or two." Technically, this was a bluff, but it felt more like a lie.

"Whaaale," Big Pops said. "That ball sure can scratch a back or two for the both of us."

"That's what I was thinking," Stewart lied again.

"Good," Big Pops said, letting go of the slip.

Stewart looked at the paper as he walked down the sidewalk to the corner to wait for the bus. Big Pops had dutifully signed 'Big Pops' on the line that said 'Big Pops' under it. Stewart thought back to his meeting the day before. Stewart was sure that the part of the Student Information Form that the principal hadn't believed was the part labeled 'Parents.'

This is what he put there:

> *Student's parents are no longer of this earth. They perished in the mysterious land of Micronesia in a tragic, unusual and confusing accident involving typhoons, bicycles, rice and Band-Aids. Student currently resides with a legal guardian, his grandfather, a.k.a 'Big Pops,' a convicted felon.*

Of course Stewart understood why the principal's mustached twitched when he read that part. It did seem hard to believe.

But, as mentioned earlier, every word of it was true.

As soon as the bus arrived that morning, Stewart had a terrible thought that made his stomach flip, flop, crawl into the very center of his body and disappear. Then his lungs froze, stopping his breathing.

While his brain tried to find his stomach and get his lungs working again, Stewart reminded it that they had some serious thinking to do.

This is the conversation he had with his organs in the two and one third seconds it took for him to climb the steps into the bus:

STEWART: Hello! Brain, we have a problem.

BRAIN: I'm aware of that. The Lungs haven't taken a breath in over five seconds.

STEWART: I'm not talking about the Lungs.

BRAIN: The Stomach is secondary. Worse that can happen there is a little vomiting.

STEWART: Forget the Stomach. Forget the Lungs. This is a *real* problem.

BRAIN: Is it Heart?

STEWART: No.

BRAIN: Thank goodness.

STEWART: I'm talking about the baseball.

BRAIN: Baseball?

STEWART: Signed by none other than Moe Berg.

BRAIN: Don't start with that. Not now. We have *real* problems here.

STEWART: This is a real problem too.

BRAIN: Oh stop.

STEWART: What if Cunningham doesn't have the baseball with him?

BRAIN: He'll have it with him.

STEWART: You don't know that.

BRAIN: Lungs? Lungs? Can you hear me? Just relax. Go to your happy place.

STEWART: Did you hear me? This is a serious problem.

BRAIN: Shhh! You're making it worse. No, Lungs, there are no serious problems. Happy place ... happy place ...

STEWART: What if Cunningham took the ball home?

BRAIN: Of course he took it home. It was in his backpack, wasn't it?

STEWART: But what if he left it at home?

BRAIN: No, no, Pancreas, I have not seen Stomach, but don't cry. We'll find him. He's just hiding somewhere. Lungs? You're not relaxing.

STEWART: How am I going to get the baseball back if Cunningham left it at home?

BRAIN: Could you maybe talk to the Eyes about this please?! They aren't doing anything right now and I'm a little bit occupied.

STEWART: Oh fine! Eyes?

EYES: We're on it.

And they were.

As soon as Stewart was heading down the aisle toward the back of the bus, his eyes spotted Cunningham in his usual seat three back from the front. They scanned the area surrounding the second biggest bully at West Plain High and locked onto the backpack sitting next to Cunningham, unzipped, on the aisle side of the seat.

Stewart heard his brain coaching his lungs to take little, shallow breaths.

BRAIN: See, Lungs? We found the backpack. And look! It's open. Eyes are just gonna peer in and check. Everything is gonna be fine. Anyone find Stomach yet?

Stewart made his way down the aisle as the bus pulled away from the curb and picked up speed. As he passed Cunningham's seat, he looked down into the open backpack.

In it he saw a notebook, some crumpled up papers and candy wrappers, two text books, a tee shirt and a few pairs of dice.

But no baseball.

BRAIN: Relax! Relax! Everyone, take it easy. Lungs, you're not breathing again. Glands, enough with the

sweating! Heart, sounds like you're playing the
drums down there. Can you please ease up? Eyes
aren't done yet.

His brain was right. Stewart's eyes immediately darted
around here and there. They zoomed in on something
moving fast, up and down.

After focusing, the something was identified as Cunningham's hand.

And there was something in it.

The baseball!

Cunningham was using the baseball to clobber the un-
lucky kid sitting in front of him.

Stewart took this fact in and kept moving toward his
usual seat in the middle of the bus next to the kid who
never spoke and wore a West Plain High sweatshirt with
the hood up over his head all the time.

On the way, his his brain reminded him how smart it
was:

BRAIN: I told you. Didn't I tell you? I told you he'd
have it with him.

STEWART: Yeah.

BRAIN: I told you.

STEWART: But how did you know?

BRAIN: Oh please. What, you think Cunningham does
homework? You think he ever opens a school book

at home? Why would he even open up his backpack?

STEWART: Oh. Right. Do you think he's gonna get
blood on the baseball, using it to beat a kid like
that?

BRAIN: Worry about that after you get it back. Which
reminds me. We need to get working on a plan.

STEWART: You're right.

BRAIN: Of course I'm right. Okay, Lungs are breathing again, Heart has slowed down, Stomach has
come out of hiding, but Glands are gonna keep
sweating for a while. Once they start, it is hard to
stop them.

Boy, was his brain ever right about that. By the time
Stewart sat down he was sporting massive pit stains on his
grey tee shirt and his forehead was slick with sweat.

Stewart didn't have time to dwell on his embarrassing
perspiration. He had a plan to hatch.

He sat perfectly still and started to think. The sound of
the school bus bouncing its way to West Plain High became background noise, barely noticeable to Stewart. And
the repetitive sound of Cunningham thwacking the kid
with his grandfather's baseball became his inspiration.

The plan hatched slowly at first. Stewart was almost
afraid of his own idea. It was crazy. It was dangerous. He
could hardly believe he dared to think it.

Then, when he realized that it just might work, and more importantly, it seemed his only hope, the hatching picked up speed and momentum, taking on a life of its own.

Finally, when the bus stopped in front of West Plain High and opened its doors, the plan burst forth fully from its shell, completely formed.

And it was one terrifying little chick.

Stewart took one quarter of a second to list the qualities he would need to exhibit in order to execute it:

Strength
Bravery
Speed
Endurance
Dexterity

He stopped there. Since he didn't naturally possess the first five required qualities, he reasoned that listing more would just depress him.

Stewart shuffled off the bus and ran through the crowd of kids heading for the doors of West Plain High so that he would be in position for the first part of his plan. He called this part Stalling Effort Phase Alpha One, or 'SEPAO' for short, or 'S' for shorter. In order to pull off 'S,' it was imperative that he get inside West Plain High before Cunningham.

He dodged and weaved between the students moseying their way to the doors.

Out of my way you sloths! he screamed in his mind.

"Excuse me please, excuse me please," he muttered out loud.

Being small has its advantages. He was able to thread his way through the crowd quickly and reached the doors twenty yards ahead of the second biggest bully at West Plain High.

He continued his weaving as he ran down the already crowded main hall. He stopped under a banner that read, 'Matthew Rollins for Student Body President.' Stewart looked at the banner carefully. He hoped he remembered correctly ... yes! One of the ties on the left side of the banner hung low enough for him to grab.

Stewart found it pleasing that 'Stalling Effort Phase Alpha One' involved the destruction of this particular banner.

Here is a transcript of a conversation he had about this banner during the first week of school with a girl whose jet black hair featured a bright pink streak down the center of it:

STEWART: Who is Matthew Rollins?
GIRL: I know, right?
STEWART: Really. Who?
GIRL: Totally.

STEWART: So he's running for President.

GIRL: Duh.

STEWART: What are his positions?

GIRL: He only has one.

STEWART: What is it?

GIRL: Quarterback.

STEWART: What is he running on?

GIRL: Sneakers I guess.

STEWART: I mean what is his platform?

GIRL: He doesn't wear platform sneakers. He's very tall.

At which point the girl realized that Stewart was actually invisible and simply walked away.

While remembering the conversation with the girl (whose hair was now neon blue), Stewart tugged on the dangling tie just as Cunningham came through the front door.

The banner broke loose and fell down across the hall, tangling up a mass of students and creating an instant pile-up as kids continued to pour through the front doors.

Stewart turned and continued down the hall. Checking over his shoulder he saw Cunningham stuck in the pile-up. Instinctively, the giant kid began flailing his arms around, smacking anyone unfortunate enough to be within his reach.

'S' accomplished. Stewart had bought himself some time.

He turned his attention to the next step in his plan, Infiltration Operation Beta One. ('I' for short.)

At the end of the main hall, he turned left into the music wing.

This is where his plan would have to start. It was the only place in the school that he saw Cunningham. There were no kids in this hall. The principal had told him no one had a first period class in the music wing. Of course that didn't explain what Cunningham had been doing down there. No matter, Stewart thought. He would solve that riddle soon enough.

Stewart headed straight for the xylophone practice room door.

Stewart assumed that this door would be locked.

He based that assumption on his belief that xylophones were valuable.

He based that belief on the fact that he had never seen a real one. He had only seen them in pictures. Specifically, in every ABC book he had ever read, as the picture for the letter 'x'. If he had never seen a real one, they could be considered rare. Rare things are often valuable.

In the four and a half seconds it took to reach the xylophone practice room door, Stewart reviewed twenty-six ways to open a locked door. Everything from the elegant 'use a set of lock picks to skillfully unlock it,' to the crude 'smash it open with a sledge hammer' crossed his mind.

But lo and behold, Stewart was wrong!

The door was unlocked. (Which was really a bit of good luck for part 'I' of the the plan because Stewart didn't have lock picks, a sledge hammer or any other things he would need to open a locked door.) He simply turned the knob, swung the door open and stepped in.

The first thing he noticed about the room was the complete lack of a xylophone in it.

Which disappointed him greatly. This seemed his best chance to see a real xylophone.

Beyond that, it confused him. A xylophone practice room without a xylophone?

He would have to think about that later. It was time to move on to Conceal and Observe Gamma One, or 'C'.

'C' was by far the craziest part of the plan. It reminded Stewart of his favorite science fiction book about a brave alien space explorer named Rotan. In it, Rotan found himself stranded on a planet populated by three-eyed, four-armed, horned creatures who harbored deep hate and resentment for all alien space explorers.

In order to escape this planet, Rotan, who himself had four arms, but just two eyes and no horns, had to sneak into the space port and hide behind barrels of space ship fuel. At just the right moment, he would leap out from behind the barrels, a laser gun in each of his four hands, blast his way onto a departing spaceship, disable the crew, take over the controls and fly home.

Upon reflection, part 'C' of his plan really wasn't that similar to the book, except that like Rotan, he would have to hide.

Stewart scanned the xylophoneless room for a place to hide. The choice was pretty easy. The only thing in the room was a tall supply cabinet. There were no tables, no chairs and, as mentioned, no xylophone. He stuffed himself into the cabinet and closed the doors behind him, hoping he would do Rotan proud.

He crouched down on the floor of the closet and prepared for Conceal and Observe Gamma Two, also know as 'C', which focused on the observing. Stewart recognized that his naming system left much to be desired. How could he differentiate Conceal and Observe Gamma One and Conceal and Observe Gamma Two by their abbreviations if both abbreviations were 'C'? Furthermore, the letters of the abbreviations did not follow a logical order and were therefore useless in determining the progress of the plan.

Stewart could have easily spent five seconds worrying about these things, and renaming each section of the plan to fix the problems, but the sound of the door to the xylophone practice room opening stopped him.

Stewart held his breath, which would prove to be a mistake.

Outside the closet, he heard someone enter the xylophone practice room. That someone was whistling. Not a tune, but a single, low note, droning on, then stopping, then starting again, always the same pitch but for different intervals. It was a song whose melody was just one note, which is to say, it was a song, but not a very good one.

From the heavy thump of the whistler's footsteps, it had to be Cunningham.

Stewart continued to hold his breath, fearing the sound of his breathing would lead to his being discovered.

Stewart heard a tremendous thud and he deduced Cunningham, still whistling, had sat himself roughly on the floor. This was followed by the sound of Cunningham's backpack zipping open.

The problem with holding your breath so as not to make a sound is that if you do it too long you will pass out. Which makes a lot of noise.

Stewart recognized the point of passing out fast approaching. He would have to take a breath.

Cunningham continued to whistle as Stewart opened his mouth to suck in some air—quietly he hoped.

Perhaps if Stewart's body regularly exercised, and therefore found being out of breath a common experience, he could have taken a slow and quiet, measured breath. But it didn't, so he couldn't. His lungs got a small taste of oxygen which overrode the need to keep quiet and took a forceful and loud swig.

Cunningham's whistling stopped.

To be discovered spying on the second biggest bully at West Plain High could not end well for him. Stewart found himself wishing he, like Rotan, had four laser guns and two extra arms.

Suddenly, there was a knock on the door to the xylophone practice room. Stewart heard Cunningham resume his one note whistle and thump his way to the door.

He heard the door open and someone stepped into the room. Cunningham greeted this person and they chatted a bit. It sounded like a student.

It seemed the bully had forgotten about hearing the gulp for air. Stewart was able to resume breathing in the closet and Part 'C' of his plan—the second 'C', the part about observing—then began in earnest. Except he couldn't really see anything in the dark supply closet. So his observing was limited to listening. Being in the closet, everything sounded muffled, so he could only catch a few words here and there, and it was difficult to know exactly what the kids in the room were doing.

He heard the door open again and more voices come into the room.

Then he heard something getting shuffled and sorted. Papers maybe?

Then he heard the sound of something bouncing and jumping. Stewart had played his share of role playing games, so he was very familiar with the sound of dice being rolled on the floor.

He was able to hear more words as the kids talked louder, even shouting sometimes.

Papers were shuffled, dice were rolled, voices shouted.

Stewart heard the muddled sound of the bell ringing in the hallway, signaling the end of first period. Then, everyone left the room except Cunningham, who started whistling the same note again. The next bell rang five minutes later, starting second period. Stewart heard the door to the xylophone practice room open again and everything happened all over.

Voices came in.

Papers were shuffled.

Dice were rolled.

Shouts were shouted.

Everyone left.

Bell rang.

During the fourth period, Stewart realized some rather serious weaknesses in his plan. Food, for example. He was getting hungry.

There was also the matter of all the classes he was missing. How was he going to explain that?

But on the bright side, he knew more about where Cunningham spent his time, and therefore where the baseball was.

He was reading the table.

During sixth period Stewart started to smell something.

Peppers and onions. And cheese. And steak. And something fried. The latest batch of voices had brought Cunningham a cheesesteak and french fries!

Oh man. Stewart was starving now. He fought off his discomfort.

This is what that fight sounded like:

STOMACH: Owwwww!

STEWART: Um, can someone quiet Stomach down
  please?

STOMACH: Grumble, grumble, grumble!

STEWART: We're gonna get caught if he keeps that up.

BRAIN: I guess you should have thought about that
  before you stuffed yourself into this closet.

STEWART: Me? Aren't you in charge of thinking?

BRAIN: Oh yeah. Sorry.

STOMACH: Awww, grumble, Owww!

BRAIN: Zip it down there!

Stewart tried to ignore his stomach pains and the smell of a hot, delicious, cheesesteak and crispy, salty and satisfying french fries by mentally compiling a list of the words and phrases he could make out in the garbled conversations he heard.

He then eliminated common words like 'hey' and 'what's up' and all the other words he heard that were small talk.

He reorganized the remaining words into an alphabetized list, hoping they would give him a clue as to what was going on in the xylophone practice room.

This is the list:

Box cars
Eleven
New shooter
Pass
Pay up
Point
Roll
Seven
Spot me

This distracted him from his growing hunger pains for all of nine seconds.

Stewart began to feel lightheaded. He had been stuck in this dark closet for hours with no food or water. He squatted down and held his knees tight to his chest trying to squeeze out the hunger pains.

He could no longer focus on part 'C' of the plan. The pain from his stomach spread through his body. Everything began to hurt. His legs from squatting, his eyes from straining in the dark, his arms from pushing himself against the back wall. The voices in the room blended with the sound of dice, Cunningham's whistling and the occasional ringing of the class bell in a skull-rattling symphony.

Until there was silence.

Stewart didn't remember hearing the last bell, but clearly, it must have rung.

Everything was quiet. There was no whistling, no voices, nothing.

His body still throbbing from hunger and stiff from his awkward pose on the floor of the closest, Stewart slowly stood back up. He carefully pushed on the closet doors.

The darkness of the closet was broken by more darkness.

The lights of the windowless xylophone practice room were off.

Stewart stepped out of the closet.

Looking around, he saw the room was once again completely empty.

He peered out the door into the music wing hallway.

Empty.

He walked down to the main hall.

Empty.

He must have passed out in the closet. The entire school was deserted.

He ran down the main hall and out the front door wondering what time it was. Seeing the sun setting gave him a clue.

Here is a list of things that Big Pops didn't seem to notice when Stewart came through the front door:

Stewart was home three hours later than usual.
Stewart arrived home on foot.
Stewart was pale and stumbling from hunger.
The school had left a message on the answering machine asking why Stewart was absent.

Here is a list of the thing Big Pops *did* notice when Stewart came through the front door an hour later:

Stewart didn't have the baseball with him.

While Stewart looked around the kitchen for dinner, Big Pops peeked into his backpack.

"Where's the baseball?" he asked.

"Um, is there dinner?" Stewart said too starving to acknowledge the complexity of Big Pops' question.

"There was," Big Pops said.

"For me?"

"Of course," Big Pops said indignantly.

"Where is it?"

"That's what I asked."

"Dinner?"

"I ate it."

"Mine?"

"That's what we're talking about, isn't it?" Big Pops asked.

Stewart stumbled to the refrigerator. The first thing he saw was a jar of pickles. His hands got busy opening it while his eyes looked for more targets.

"So how's about my question," Big Pops said. "The baseball?"

"Ibts whaaach abooo mee quelfs," Stewart said with two dills stuffed in his mouth.

"Huh?"

"It's 'what about my question?'" Stewart repeated after swallowing.

"What are you asking me for?" Big Pops asked.

"I wasn't."

"I understand," Big Pops said, which surprised Stewart for several reasons. "Hard to stop being cool, isn't it?"

"Ifb fuure iz," Stewart said, his mouth now filled with leftover pasta.

"Whaaale," Big Pops said. "The cogs are spinning on a fine solution there for sure. I'll fill you in on it tomorrow."

Stewart moved on to the pantry to gorge on some dry cereal while Big Pops went back to play more online poker.

Online poker.

That got Stewart to thinking. He continued thinking while he gorged. Being worn out and sore from both his time in the closet and the four mile walk home, and having no homework since he missed all his classes, Stewart got himself ready for bed, thinking the whole time.

When he climbed under his sheets, he finished thinking and had reached a conclusion. Big Pops would know what all the words he heard in the xylophone practice room meant. He based this conclusion on the similarity of those words to words Big Pops used while playing online poker.

Stewart decided that he would ask Big Pops about it when his grandfather came in to tuck him in.

Oh.

He forgot.

Big Pops didn't do that.

Stewart hadn't been tucked in since the night before his parents left for Micronesia.

So Stewart got out of bed and hobbled his way into the TV room. He waited for Big Pops to be done with a hand of poker, then recited the words on his mental list and asked what they might mean.

"Craps," Big Pops said.

Stewart patiently waited.

"Why you staring at me?" Big Pops asked after two minutes of this.

"Oh," Stewart said, surprised. "I was waiting for an answer."

"You didn't hear me?" Big Pops asked.

"I heard you."

"What'd I say?"

"I can't say," Stewart said.

"Why not?"

"It's a bad word."

"No," Big Pops said, reaching for a book on a stack beside his recliner. "It's a game."

He handed the book to Stewart. On the cover was a pair of rolling red dice under the title.

"How to Win at Craps'" he read, giggling because he never said a bad word before.

Stewart had moved in with Big Pops during summer break, three weeks before school started. They spent a lot of time playing poker.

Stewart was more used to online role playing computer games with magic, sword fighting and fire-breathing dragons. These were complicated games played with thousands of other kids that he would never meet in person. So at first, the idea of playing a game, face to face with someone, with nothing more than cards, seemed odd to him. Making it stranger still was the fact that he was face to face with Big Pops, his father's father, a direct relative Stewart didn't know at all on account of prison. So at first he didn't even want to play. This is a transcript of Big Pops' first efforts to get his grandson to play poker with him:

BIG POPS: You got any money?

STEWART: Um, I guess. Some.

BIG POPS: Let's play poker.

STEWART: For money?

BIG POPS: Of course.

STEWART: I don't know how to play.

BIG POPS: I'll teach you.

STEWART: I don't want to play.

BIG POPS: Sure you do.

STEWART: I ... no, I just want—

BIG POPS: I'll deal.

STEWART: What if I lose all my money?

BIG POPS: Whaaale, a fly in the ointment now and
then don't change the color of the leopards spot's.
Pick up your cards.

As you can see, Big Pops is nothing if not persistent.

His motives were pure.

Well, half pure.

The pure half was trying to distract Stewart, who obviously had a lot on his mind. His parents were not coming home from Micronesia. He was living with Big Pops now. The kid, Big Pops reasoned, needed to think about something else for a while. Why not poker?

The not so pure half was driven by the fact that Big Pops really liked poker and he hadn't played a good poker game since he was let out of prison.

Eventually, Big Pops' persistence won out and Stewart sat down to learn how to play poker from his grandfather, the felon. At first, these games were uncomfortable and scary for Stewart. But he had a curious mind and liked learning new things, so eventually discomfort and fear gave way to interest and enjoyment.

STEWART: Let's play pot limit Texas Hold 'em, with
options to run it twice.

BIG POPS: Kid's a natural!

And in a matter of days, he got quite good at it.

STEWART: Big Pops, you don't have to pay me that money you owe for poker.
BIG POPS: I'm no welsher. How much is it again?
STEWART: One thousand three hundred and fifty dollars.
BIG POPS: Um …

Just when he was starting to enjoy playing poker with Big Pops, Stewart made, in poker terms, a huge blunder.

STEWART: Big Pops, did you know you can play poker online?
BIG POPS: Where is online?
STEWART: On the computer.
BIG POPS: Against a computer?
STEWART: Against people. On the computer.
BIG POPS: For money?

So Big Pops started poker playing online. He quickly realized the people playing online weren't nearly as good as his grandson. That meant the games weren't as fun. But it also meant he could win.

After playing online for just three nights he won enough money to pay back Stewart the incredible sum of one thousand three hundred and fifty dollars. Then he continued playing online virtually nonstop.

Stewart had grown to really enjoy the poker games with Big Pops. It did take his mind off other things. And he really liked the game itself. Poker had a mix of mathematics and dramatics. A good player had to determine probabilities, calculate rates of return and remember odds. But they also had to pretend like they had a good hand when they had a bad one, and pretend like they had a bad one when they had a good one. Or better yet, pretend like they didn't care one way or the other. And you had to read the table, figure out what your opponents were doing and make a plan to beat them.

At that particular time, living with a grandfather he hardly knew, getting ready to start a new school and still missing his parents, pretending he didn't care one way or the other about things felt pretty good.

But when Big Pops became obsessed with online poker, things for Stewart went back to the way they were when he first moved in. He spent a lot of time in his room, feeling uncomfortable and sad.

At least he had one thousand three hundred and fifty dollars, though. All of which he had stuffed into two big wads in the front pockets of his jeans Wednesday morning as he limped his way outside to catch the bus, still sore from Tuesday's adventures.

As the bus bounced along, Stewart read the book on craps that Big Pops had lent him. He took in the dice game with his typical sponge-like ability to learn and retain information, the same ability that had lead to his poker success.

By the time the bus stopped in front of school, Stewart knew enough about craps to consider himself proficient at it, even though he had never played it once. Which was good, because being good at craps was crucial to his next plan.

Stewart considered this plan to be much better than his last plan.

Here is a list of differences:

There is no hiding involved.
He did not expect to get overly sore executing this
  plan.
This plan started after a good lunch.
This plan would be complete long before his bus left
  for home.
This plan would not be broken down into parts with
  confusing names that didn't follow alphabetical
  order.

Here is a list of similarities:

This plan also required bravery that bordered on stupidity.

Stewart secretly continued to study *How to Win at Craps* during his morning classes. If he was proficient when he got to school that morning, by the end of geometry he was an expert. He had one more class, then lunch, then a free study period during sixth period, at which time he would execute this new plan. Stewart would go to the xylophone practice room and play craps with Cunningham, the second biggest bully at West Plain High, for his grandfather's baseball.

During that last class before lunch, science, he put the craps book away. There was nothing left for him to learn from it. He knew he could beat Cunningham.

Little did he know that his decision to pay attention to the slide show about global warming instead of reading a book about betting on dice would lead to disaster.

The first few slides showed factories belching smoke into the atmosphere, highways congested with cars and forests being turned into fields as their trees were harvested. The teacher talked about the possibility of human activity contributing to global warming.

The next few slides showed some of the effects of global warming. There was a picture of the side of a glacier falling into the sea, a graph showing the rise in temperatures through time and a map of the world's coast lines, with a bright red line predicting their rise.

There was nothing here that Stewart didn't know already, and none of the slides to the that point surprised him.

But the next one did.

It was a picture of a tornado.

Huh, Stewart thought to himself. *A tornado.*

The teacher explained that some scientists thought there was a connection between global warming and extreme weather patterns. Stewart didn't know that. His attention was fully focused on the slide show.

The next image was of a flooded home. Muddy water from a nearby stream washed into a white house while rain poured down on the scene.

Huh. Flooding.

The next slide showed a satellite image of a hurricane hovering over the state of Florida.

Huh, thought Stewart. *A hurricane.* He felt a tingle on the back of this neck.

Then there was a picture of a beach town ravaged by a tsunami. The teacher said that the countries in the Pacific Ocean were particularly susceptible to tsunamis.

Huh. Pacific Ocean.

Stewart felt dizzy.

The next slide was of a rain-filled storm battering a tropical island. Palm trees bent sideways in the wind, water filled the streets. Waves were crashing on the beach.

The teacher explained that storms of this magnitude were called hurricanes when they developed in the Atlantic Ocean. When they developed in the Pacific Ocean, they were called typhoons.

Stewart started to think, *huh,* made it to *hu* ..., passed out and fell to the floor of his science class.

Stewart didn't forget many things. Hardly anything really. But one thing he knew he would never forget as long as he lived was the first feeling he was aware of when he regained consciousness in the nurses office an hour later.

Actually, the first feeling he was aware of felt like someone poking him in the stomach with a tongue depressor. Which was exactly what the nurse was doing to him. And the second feeling was a mixture of a headache (from the fall) and hunger (from missing lunch).

He wouldn't forget those two feelings either, but for no reason more significant than Stewart didn't forget many things.

The third feeling was the one that mattered, the one he didn't want to forget—ever. It was the feeling he tried to explain to the nurse as she poked Stewart in the stomach with a tongue depressor.

Here is a transcript of his effort:

STEWART: I am connected to the Pacific Ocean.

NURSE: You gonna puke?

STEWART: And the Pacific Ocean is connected to typhoons.

NURSE: Are you?

STEWART: And I am connected to typhoons.

NURSE: Okay.

STEWART: And typhoons are connected to bicycles.

NURSE: Uh-huh.

STEWART: Why are you poking me with that?

NURSE: In case you puke.

STEWART: Why would I puke?

NURSE: Kids come down here always puke.

STEWART: Don't you think poking me in the stomach will me puke?

NURSE: That's the idea. Get it over with.

At that point, Stewart decided to explain the feeling to himself instead while he laid on the nurses examination table and she continued to poke him.

I am connected to the Pacific Ocean, he said to himself, even though he didn't know exactly what he meant by that.

The Pacific Ocean is connected to typhoons.

I am connected to typhoons.

Typhoons are connected to bicycles.

Bicycles are connected to Micronesia.

Bicycles are connected to global warming.

My mother is connected to bicycles.

My father is connected to bicycles.

I am connected to bicycles.

My mother is connected to Micronesia and my father and the Pacific Ocean and typhoons and global warming and me.

He was crying now.

The nurse assumed that meant he was on the verge of puking, and so she jabbed him harder and faster.

But he wasn't going to puke.

He was crying because he was connected.

He was connected to geography, to the Pacific Ocean, to global warming, typhoons, to bicycles, to Micronesia, to his mother, to his father, to Big Pops, to Moe Berg ...

Moe Berg? Stewart wondered.

How did he get in there?

Moe Berg!

Stewart leaped to his feet.

"What time is it?" Stewart asked, panicked.

"Puke time?" the nurse tried.

"What period is it?"

"Sixth just started."

Perfect! He still had time. The plan wasn't ruined.

After promising the nurse he would not puke, he left her office and headed down the hall.

As he ran toward the music wing, he took stock of himself.

He was limping slightly from his sore muscles, his head was ringing from falling on the floor, his stomach hurt from being poked by a tongue depressor, he was starving again from missing lunch and he had a vague feeling of connectedness.

This last feeling was the only one he liked. He didn't know exactly what is was, or why it made him pass out, or why it felt good to him now. But he hoped it would last.

It didn't.

As he approached the door to the xylophone practice room, Stewart was bumped violently from behind by a kid jogging toward the same door.

The feeling of connectedness was replaced by a more familiar feeling of falling.

He hit the ground hard and let out a grunt.

From the ground, he watched his assailant continue on to the xylophone practice room, opened the door and let himself in, never looking back.

Invisible again, Stewart thought, picking his bruised and battered body off the floor.

He limped his way to the door, took a deep breath, rallied his courage, opened the door and stepped into the xylophone practice room.

Here is a transcript of Stewart's initial reaction to what he saw:

STEWART: Holy cow! This place is packed! Jeez! There must be twenty kids in here! And they're all gambling. How can so many kids know about this game? Wow! Look at all the money they are betting. And look at all the money in his hand. There must be five hundred dollars in his fist. And this is just one period. Games like this go on all day! Cunningham must be making a fortune! Boy, it's really loud in here. I can't believe he hasn't got—

The transcript ends suddenly because Stewart realized everyone in the xylophone practice room was staring at him.

Clearly, he was no longer invisible.

All the students were hunched in a circle around the the center of the room, their heads twisted to face Stewart.

He knew they were all thinking, 'Who is this geek and what is he doing here?' or some variation of that.

At the far end of the circle, Cunningham stared at Stewart. He didn't look pleased to have his game interrupted.

Stewart defensively dug his wads of cash out of his front pockets and held them up.

"I'm here to play craps," he said timidly.

Cunningham's broad face broke into a grin when he saw all of Stewart's cash. With a grunt, Cunningham acknowledged Stewart and therefore granted him access to the game.

Instinctively, the other kids shifted around, making room for Stewart in the circle.

These are the basic rules of craps:

A player called the 'shooter' rolls a pair of dice until they win or lose their turn.

If the shooter rolls a 7 or 11 on their first roll, they win their turn.

If the shooter rolls 2, 3 or a 12 on their first roll, they lose their turn.

If the shooter rolls a 4, 5, 6, 8, 9 or 10 on their first roll, that number becomes their 'point.'

The shooter rolls the dice again.

If they roll their point, they win their turn.

If they roll a 7, they lose their turn.

If they roll a different number they roll again.

Other players can bet on the shooter, chancing that he will win his turn.

If the shooter wins their turn they, and the players who bet with the shooter, win their bet.

If they lose their turn, the 'house,' in this case Cunningham, wins the money the players wagered.

The current shooter was a girl Stewart recognized from his Chemistry class. All the other kids in the circle put money in front of the them. Some put a dollar, others a few dollars. Stewart saw one kid put down a ten dollar bill.

He pulled a five from his wad and placed it on the ground in front of him like the other kids.

The shooter rolled an 11.

Winner!

Everyone in the circle hooted and screamed in excitement.

"Yes!" someone screamed.

"Pay out Cunningham!" someone else shouted, which seemed pretty dangerous to Stewart.

But the second biggest bully at West Plain High seemed to take the loss in stride. He even chuckled a little as he passed out money from his pile, paying off all the kid's bets.

When you win your turn in craps you get to roll again. So the girl picked up the dice and shook them in her hand while everyone made their new bets.

Stewart again bet five dollars.

The shooter rolled an 8.

That was her 'point.' If she rolled an 8 again before rolling a 7, everyone would win.

In the amount of time it took the shooter to pick up the dice and get ready to roll again, Stewart calculated the chances of rolling an 8 as 5 out of 36, or 13.89%, and the chances of rolling a 7 as 6 out of 36, or 16.67%. He recognized that the 7 was more likely, but he was caught up in the excitement of the game and couldn't help thinking the players would win again.

He was wrong.

The shooter rolled a 7.

Everyone in the circle moaned as Cunningham collected his winnings.

The dice were passed to a new shooter and the game continued.

In his mind, Stewart kept track of the points, the wins and losses and the statistical consistencies with standard probabilities, making several meaningful observations as well as constructing a hypothesis or two about craps in general and this game in particular.

He did this purely for entertainment.

That's just the kind of wild guy he was.

He didn't really care if he, or the other players, won or lost. All he cared about was becoming the shooter so he could propose a bet to Cunningham. After one more roll, which the house won again, the dice were thrust into his hands. It was time for the next step in his plan.

"Ahem," he said to no one in particular and no one at all noticed.

"Ahem!" he said again, much louder and this time everyone noticed. And they didn't like it. Stewart once again found himself being stared at by everyone in the room. This time the unspoken question clearly was, 'Why isn't this geek rolling the dice?'

Straining to stay the course and execute the plan, Stewart locked eyes with Cunningham. A chill ran down his neck as his mind registered just how big Cunningham was.

He knew he might not get the dice again. This was his only chance to slow the game down enough to propose a special bet. He mustered his courage and spoke.

"Well, I don't know about you guys," Stewart said with a quiver in his voice. "But I don't need any more money."

There were three things wrong with this statement.

The first was that Stewart had the audacity to strike a familiar tone with the rest of the players. Who did he think he was? The second was that he was speaking gibberish. Who doesn't need any more money? What was he talking about?

The third was that he wasn't rolling the dice.

The faces in the circle furrowed their brows and pursed their lips. But for the second time that afternoon, Cunningham grunted his approval, prompting Stewart to continue.

"How about I put up my money and you put up something else?" Stewart asked Cunningham, the House.

Cunningham shrugged his shoulders.

"Like your backpack," Stewart suggested, placing a ten dollar bill on the ground.

Cunningham slowly shook his head.

Stewart placed a twenty on top of the ten.

Cunningham shrugged.

Stewart placed another twenty down.

Cunningham nodded his head.

The bet was on.

Stewart's fifty dollars cash against Cunningham's back-pack.

Of course, Stewart didn't want the backpack. He wanted what was in it.

Stewart rolled the dice.

9. That became his point.

Cunningham handed him the dice. He shook them and rolled.

7.

He lost.

Cunningham scooped up the fifty dollars and passed the dice to the next shooter. Everyone in the circle placed their bets again.

"Again for the backpack?" Stewart asked Cunningham, putting another fifty dollars down. Cunningham nodded, the shooter rolled.

He didn't care at all that he just lost fifty dollars. The important thing was that the bet for the backpack had been established and could be made again and again. If he were explain to you why this was important, this is what he would say:

STEWART: While it is a certainty that over a great
number of games, the house maintains a slim advantage (less than 2%!), this typical analysis is moot
for the purposes of my plan because I am not interested in accruing long term, consistent wins for the
purpose of accumulating money. Mine is a quest for
a 'threshold' event, one which, once crossed, means
victory. In other words, the long term effects of the
house odds advantage is irrelevant to the task at
hand. And while it is very true that dice have no
memory, and taken as individual events—which
they are—each roll of the dice favors the house, statistical thinking does allow us to consider more than
one as a group when conditions are such that the
group must be considered as such. The seeking of a
threshold event demands such consideration.

To which you might say, 'What?'

This is what someone who wanted you to understand all
that would say:

SOMEONE: Now that they were betting for the backpack, Stewart only needed to win once. And he had
plenty of money to keep trying.

The new shooter rolled. The point became 5. Cunningham handed the shooter the dice again.

7.

The money was scooped, the dice were passed, the bet was repeated, the shooter rolled.

10. Then 7.

This remarkable string of bad luck for the players didn't bother Stewart. With his impressive bankroll, Stewart could afford to make this bet at least twenty-six times. All he had to do was win once. In fact, he was intrigued by the pattern developing in the roles of the dice.

Next shooter.

8 then 7.

Next shooter.

5 then 7.

Next shooter.

6 then 7.

This is astounding! Stewart marveled to himself. *The probability of all these 7's being rolled in such a unique pattern. Every other number is a 7! I am witnessing something very incredible here.*

Next shooter.

9 then 7.

And then the bell rang.

The circle of kids broke up and left the xylophone practice room, all quite a bit poorer. Stewart went with them, grinning at the mathematically improbable event he just witnessed.

The precise pattern he had witnessed was incredible. A 7 had been rolled every other throw of the dice for fourteen rolls in a row. This of course was much more improbable that just rolling a 7 seven times in a row (the odds of which were 1 in 279,936). The fact that a seven was never rolled twice in a row made the odds of what just happened a staggering 1 in 1,003,061!

Of course Stewart realized that had a 7 been rolled twice in a row, he would have won because rolling a 7 on the first roll of a turn means the players win. But that fact seemed hardly interesting to him just then. As he headed to his next class, he compiled a list of highly unlikely things that were more likely to happen than the pattern he just witnessed.

Here are some highlights from that lists:

It was more likely that Stewart would be struck by lightning.

It was more likely that Stewart would win an Olympic Medal.

It was more likely that the Earth would get hit by an asteroid in the next one hundred years.

It was more likely that 3 letters chosen at random would form a word or name, like 'Moe.'

It was more likely that 4 letters chosen at random would form a word or name like 'Berg.'

Stewart thought about those last two items as he sat down for English class.

Moe.

Berg.

Huh.

Moe Berg!

Stewart got so caught up in the mathematical impossibility of what was happening that he forget the very basic premise of his plan. All he had to do was stay until he won *once* and he would have the baseball back. All he had to do was stay and keep betting. He would have to win once.

He would have to.

For the rest of the school day while his teachers taught him things he already knew, Stewart rolled three questions around in his head:

Why did he leave with the rest of the players when he should have stayed until he won?

What were the odds that he would have kept losing until he lost all his money?

What does the term 'mathematical impossibility' mean?

By the end of the school day, he was starving again after missing lunch for the second day in a row. His body sore and bruised, he limped his way onto the bus while his mind answered two of the questions.

He left with the other players simply because they left. It had taken him a lot of courage to enter the xylophone practice room and get himself into the game. And when the other players accepted him, or at least tolerated his presence, it felt, well, nice. Stewart deduced that subconsciously he wanted that feeling of acceptance to continue and therefore, without rational thought, he simply got up like they did and left like they did so he could be like them for just a few seconds more.

Pretty pathetic, he knew. But likely accurate.

As for the second question, 1 in 140,168,339,535,-626,000.

Which left the phrase 'mathematical impossibility.'

He knew he would have to talk to Big Pops about this. Not because Big Pops understood mathematics, but because Big Pops understood gambling.

The trick of course would be to talk to Big Pops without talking about his baseball.

That trick was made harder by the exhaustion Stewart felt after having to limp home for the second day in a row. Shortly after pulling out of West Plain High, Stewart's bus got a flat tire.

The driver, claiming to be going for help, flagged down a passing car, got in and drove off. After waiting for an hour for his return, the students gave up and set out for home on foot.

Stewart, gasping, sore and starving, stumbled through the front door.

This time, Big Pops was waiting for him in the kitchen with a hot dinner of chicken and french fries waiting for him.

Stewart sat at the table and dove in.

"Enjoy," Big Pops said, watching him.

"Messa plumpf," Stewart said through a mouth full of food.

It was weird that Big Pops cooked dinner for him. Meals were usually somewhere between a combined effort and an individual scavenger hunt.

It was weird that Big Pops wasn't playing online poker.

It was weird that Big Pops was staring at Stewart the whole time he was eating.

A lot of weird things were going on and it was making Stewart feel a little weird. That was probably why after he pushed his empty plate away and leaned back in his chair he hesitated before asking Big Pops about the craps game, which would prove to be a costly mistake. Had he started the conversation himself, perhaps he could have kept control of it and kept Big Pops from asking what he asked right away during Stewart's moment of hesitation.

"Where's the baseball?"

"Ahhh," Stewart stalled.

"Well?" Big Pops asked sharply.

Stewart decided to bluff again.

"It's in my backpack," he said confidently.

"Good," Big Pops said. "Give it to me."

So much for that bluff.

"It's not in my backpack," Stewart said.

Big Pops nodded his head slowly and pulled his hand back.

"Let me ask you something," Big Pops said. He paused, scratched his neck and looked at the ceiling before continuing. "I was in prison."

Stewart realized that wasn't a question, but decided not to correct Big Pops. Instead, he nodded his head.

"Do you know why I was in prison?"

That was a question. Stewart shook his head.

"Your folks never told you?"

Stewart shook his head again.

Big Pops looked at the ceiling again, frowning, then lowered his gaze, aiming his squinting eyes right at Stewart.

"You know why people get thrown into prison?"

Stewart nodded.

"You get thrown in prison for doing things that they think are bad," Big Pops continued, even though Stewart knew that one. "You know who 'they' are, the ones that do the throwing?"

Stewart nodded again. He knew this one too.

"They are the lawmakers and the cops," Big Pops said. "You sure you don't know why they threw me in prison?"

Stewart nodded.

"You want to guess?"

Stewart shook his head.

"Must have been something they thought was bad, right?"

Stewart nodded.

Big Pops nodded too.

"Whaaale, sometimes the guy who has the keys gets to fly the airplane," he said laughing.

Stewart laughed too because it seemed like he should.

"They got it wrong," Big Pops continued. "It's nothing to be ashamed of. It's a skill really, what I do. See what I mean?"

Stewart nodded even though he didn't.

"You bring me that baseball," his grandfather told him.

Stewart was stunned into silence by this conversation. He had seen his fair share of movies rated PG-13. He knew what veiled threats of violence sounded like.

"You wanted to ask me something?" Big Pops asked.

"Huh?" Stewart grunted.

"You had a question?"

Stewart figured he might as well ask him about the craps game even though it seemed Big Pops might kill him tomorrow if he didn't get the baseball back.

So he told his grandfather about the craps game and the incredible string of rolls he witnessed.

"Have you ever seen anything like that?" Stewart asked.

"Oh sure," Big Pops said. "Lots of times."

Stewart's jaw dropped as incredible odds calculations spun wildly through his mind.

"How is that possible?" he asked.

Big Pops shrugged.

"Loaded dice."

Stewart woke up before sunrise, sore, tired and hungry.

He was sore from walking home two days in a row after spending an entire day stuffed in a closet.

He was tired because he stayed awake all night thinking about loaded dice, Moe Berg and Big Pops.

He was hungry because at midnight he threw up his chicken dinner.

Here is how that happened:

Thinking about loaded dice made him think about Cunningham.

Thinking about Cunningham made him think about the baseball.

Thinking about the baseball made him think about Big Pops.

Thinking about Big Pops made him think about Big Pops talking about jail.

Thinking about Big Pops talking about jail made him think about Big Pops telling him to bring the ball back.

Thinking about Big Pops telling him to bring the ball back made him wonder what Big Pops would do to him if he didn't bring the ball back.

Wondering what Big Pops would do to him if he didn't bring the ball back made him wonder what Big Pops did to end up in jail.

*Wondering what Big Pops did to end up in jail made
him realize he better bring the ball back.
Thinking about getting the ball back made him wonder how he was going to get the ball back.
Thinking about how he was going to get the baseball
back made him think about loaded dice.*

The cycle would repeat again and again, faster and
faster, making him more and more upset, worried and
afraid until his stomach tried to squeeze back into its hiding place. Being filled with chicken, it couldn't fit. So his
stomach solved that problem by throwing up.

He snuck through the kitchen, to the side door of the
house, looking longingly at the refrigerator. He wanted
nothing more than to fry up some pork roll, sit his body
down and devour it.

But he couldn't risk waking up Big Pops. He was sneaking out of the house before dawn so he wouldn't have to
face his grandfather. He sat himself down on the curb at
the end of the street and rummaged though his backpack.
He found a few broken Lifesavers and half of a stale
cookie.

That would have to do for breakfast.

Waiting for the sun to rise, and then for the bus to come
an hour later, Stewart had plenty of time to formulate a
new plan. In fact, given Stewart's lightning fast thinking

and the large amount of time on his hands, Stewart could have formulated a hundred plans.

He could have then forgotten the first hundred, come up with another hundred, then compared that to the first hundred (because he never really forgot anything) and check for duplicates.

But nothing came to mind.

Not a thing.

He just couldn't get over the fact that the game was fixed. Cunningham was using loaded dice.

'Loaded dice' are dice that have been rigged to roll specific numbers, usually by adding weight to one side. They are used to cheat the other players. In this instance, Cunningham must have switched from regular dice to dice loaded to roll a seven every time he needed the shooter to lose.

He found the whole thing depressing.

It's not that, on a different day, he couldn't have come up with a plan for dealing with loaded dice. It's just that he couldn't on that day.

He was out of steam.

No matter how many times he reminded himself how important it was that he come up with something, he just stared off down the street.

Here is a transcript of his thoughts:

STEWART: Come on, Brain. Think.

BRAIN: I don't wanna.

STEWART: It's important!

BRAIN: I don't wanna.

STEWART: You have to.

STOMACH: I'm hungry!

STEWART: Stomach, I'm not talking to you.

LEGS: We're sore!

STEWART: Stop complaining. A little exercise is good for you.

STOMACH: I'm so hungry—

STEWART: If you hadn't thrown up that chicken —

BRAIN: Can you guys keep it down? I'm trying to rest.

STEWART: You're supposed to be thinking!

BRAIN: I don't wanna.

This bickering went on and on in his head. Eventually the birds woke up and started tweeting and whistling, the sun slowly rose, lighting up the street that his bus finally drove down.

It stopped in front of Stewart sitting on the curb.

Slowly, with his legs screaming the whole way, he hauled himself up and marched grimly onto the bus.

The bus driver, clearly annoyed at Stewart's slow pace, slammed the door shut and gunned the engine. The bus took off with a jolt, sending Stewart bouncing down the aisle.

His tired legs failed him and he tipped over and stumbled onto a kid's lap.

That kid was Cunningham.

Stewart was sprawled out across Cunningham's knees on his back looking up at the second biggest bully at West Plain High. Stewart thrashed wildly, trying to get up. But the weight of his backpack kept him down. His sore limbs couldn't muster the strength to get him up. He couldn't do anything but stare up at Cunningham with wide eyes that were prepared to be punched.

Oddly, they weren't.

Even odder was what they saw. Cunningham was smiling down at Stewart.

Odder still was what Cunningham said to Stewart.

"Nice to see you," the bully grunted. "Dice today?"

Cunningham helped him to his feet. Stewart said thanks and made his way back to his usual seat.

After Stewart calmed down, he realized that of course Cunningham wouldn't punch him. He wanted Stewart unhurt and ready to play craps. He had won a lot of money from Stewart yesterday and hoped to again today.

'Won' wasn't quite the right word. 'Took' was more like it. Cheating with stolen dice was just like stealing really.

Then another odd thing happened to Stewart, one that would be harder for him to explain. The kid who sat next to him on the bus, the one who always wore his sweatshirt hood up, hiding his face, started talking to Stewart.

"Hey," he said, tilting his covered head toward Stewart. "Hey you."

Stewart was shocked. Though he had sat next to this boy every day since school started, he didn't know his name, had never heard his voice or even seen his face.

"Who, me?" Stewart asked.

"Yeah, you," the kid said. Then he got right down to business. "I understand you lost a little money yesterday."

"Huh?" Stewart said, surprised. "How did you know that?"

"Don't worry about how I know that," his seat mate told him sternly. "Just that I do is all that matters. You know that game is fixed?"

"I do now."

"Uh huh. What do you want to do about that?"

"Ah, well … um …," Stewart stammered, still shaken by the whole conversation.

"You want to win, right?" the hooded kid asked. "You don't go into that room if you don't want to win."

"Yes, but—" Stewart wanted to explain that he didn't want to win money, but rather the baseball, signed by none other than Moe Berg.

"We don't have a lot of time here," the kid cut him off. "You want to win. Enough said. I got ways to make that happen. Meet me in the stairwell by the gym. Fifth period."

"Fifth period?" Stewart asked, thinking of his grumbling stomach. "That's my lunch."

"Lunch? Forget it," the kid said sternly. "You want to take down Cunningham's little game? You want to win? Meet me. We'll go over some things. Got it?"

Stewart considered the hooded kid carefully, wondering what he had in mind. The kid didn't look much bigger than Stewart, so he must not have been planning on fighting the second biggest bully at West Plain High. He must have had a plan to cheat the cheater.

And ultimately, that's what made Stewart nod his head, giving up his desperately needed lunch. He had no plan to get the baseball back but his seat mate evidently did.

"Got it," he said as the bus stopped in front of the school.

Stewart spent the first four morning classes ignoring his teachers, thinking about the encounter on the bus. Who was the kid in the hooded sweatshirt? How did he know Stewart played craps yesterday? And how did he know he lost? How would he beat Cunningham? And why would he talk to Stewart about it?

He was able to convince his exhausted brain to ignore the complaints of his starving stomach and do a little thinking on the subject. By the time he made his way to the stairwell by the gym, he had a few ideas about what his mysterious ally had in mind.

"You're going to switch the dice on him, aren't you?" Stewart blurted out without so much as a hello.

"Hold on," his seat mate said, hood still up over his head.

"Or you're going to tamper with the loaded dice."

"Hold on."

"That's got to be it," Stewart continued. "There's no other way to win."

"You got the right idea there but—"

"I knew it! So what's the plan? You want me to create a diversion while you switch the dice?"

"Wait a second, you got to slow down here," the kid said. But Stewart couldn't. His curious mind was as hungry for information as his stomach was for food.

"Will the dice you switch to be loaded too?" Stewart asked. "Or are we going to take our chances? I've got the money."

"Speaking of money, I hear you got a lot."

"I do," Stewart told him. "But I have to tell you, I don't care about winning money."

"Huh?" the kid asked.

So Stewart told him what he was after. The kid in the sweatshirt didn't know what to make of it. He just shook his head and shrugged.

"So, you don't care about the money," he asked Stewart. "But you got that big wad of cash with you, right?"

"Yes."

"I'm gonna need that."

"You?"

"Sure."

"Ah! I'm gonna front you the money and you're going to switch the dice and win!"

"Kind of."

"That reminds me," Stewart said, his curiosity still hungry. "How did you know about that? About all my money? And that I played craps yesterday?"

"I got people. They tell me things."

"And that reminds me, why do you want to help me anyway? And that reminds me, who are you?"

"Cool it, man!" the kid snapped, silencing Stewart. He looked at the ground, thinking for a minute. "Okay, fine. You really want to know, I'll tell you."

With that the kid pulled his hood down, showing his face for the first time. He pointed at his face, obviously expecting Stewart to recognize him.

"Huh?" the kid said. Stewart just stared at him. "Nothing? You don't know?"

Stewart shook his head slowly.

"I'm Freddy."

"Freddy?" Stewart asked.

"Dead-y Freddy," Freddy said. "The bully."

"Oh," Stewart said, pretending to recognize him.

"You really don't know who I am?"

"I'm new this year."

"Oh," Freddy said. "That explains it."

"So you're a bully?"

"Not *a* bully. *The* bully," Freddy said. "The biggest bully at West Plain High."

"Oh, because Cunningham is the—" Stewart started.

"—second biggest." Freddy finished.

"I was wondering who the first biggest was."

"Now you know."

"Um, Freddy," Stewart said, looking Freddy up and down. "Don't take this the wrong way, but you aren't much bigger than me."

"Yeah, well, I used to be," Freddy said.

"What happened?"

"Camp Lose-a-lot."

"What's that?"

" A place your parents send you over the summer to lose weight," Freddy said reluctantly.

"Well, you look good," Stewart said because he could tell Freddy felt a little weird about this revelation.

"Well, thanks," Freddy said quietly. "That's nice to hear."

There was an awkward pause, then Freddy clapped his hands and rubbed them together, changing the mood.

"So anyway," he said. "I'm mounting a comeback."

"A comeback?" Stewart asked.

"In the bully business," Freddy explained. "I'm lacking the advantage of size, so I'm gonna be a new kind of bully."

"Interesting."

"Cunning. Smart. Clever," Freddy said. "And I'm starting today."

"That's exciting."

"So, you got the money?" Freddy asked, hand extended.

"Yes, but—" Stewart started. He still wanted to hear more about the plan for winning the crooked game of craps.

"Bah!" Freddy stopped him with a raised palm. "The money?"

"But—"

"The money," Freddy said quieter and more intensely.

Stewart sighed, and reached into his pockets. He handed over his remaining cash, one thousand dollars.

"So you want to meet me at the xylophone practice room?" Stewart asked.

"Ah, yeah," Freddy said, counting the cash. "Xylophone room ... right."

"Sixth period, right?"

"Sixth, right."

"I'l be staking you, and you'll switch the dice, right?"

"Stake, switch, yeah," Freddy mumbled, heading for the stairs.

"I'll meet you in the music wing!" Stewart called to him.

Stewart found Freddy's reply curious.

"I'm back!" the first biggest bully at West Plain High shouted as he disappeared up the stairs.

As soon as he got to the music wing, Stewart's brain started asking questions.

BRAIN: Something just doesn't make sense here.
STEWART: Oh stop worrying.
BRAIN: I'm just saying ...
STEWART: What?
BRAIN: I'm not sure. If I wasn't so tired, I could figure out what's bugging me.
STEWART: What's bugging me is, I'm starving.
STOMACH: I said sorry already for throwing up, Can you get off my back?
BACK: Someone looking for me?
STEWART: Brain, relax. We're lucky. We've found someone to help us. A bully no less. Biggest bully at West Plain High.

Stewart paced the hall in front of the door to the xylophone practice room waiting for Freddy. Kids came down the hall, heading for the craps game, knocking Stewart this way and that, because of course, he was invisible to them.

After waiting for ten minutes, his brain got agitated.

BRAIN: Admit it!
STEWART: Admit what?
BRAIN: You thought it was weird.
STEWART: I don't know what you are talking about.

BRAIN: Oh stop.

STEWART: What?

BRAIN: Of course you know what I'm talking about. I'm your brain!

STEWART: Fine, it was a little weird.

BRAIN: Why did he say that?

STEWART: Yeah …

STOMACH: What are you guys talking about?

BRAIN: What did Freddy mean when he said, 'He's back.'

STOMACH: Oh, that.

STEWART: Stop it. We're gonna get the baseball—

BRAIN: —signed by none other than Moe Berg—

STEWART: —so just relax.

STOMACH: Who is Moe Berg anyway?

BRAIN: Good question.

Stewart found that if he leaned against the wall, he wouldn't get bumped into by kids coming and going from the craps game. As they passed by, he'd occasionally nod his head, maybe even give them a 'Hey,' but he remained invisible.

Another ten minutes went by.

STOMACH: Hey guys!

STEWART: I know you're hungry.

STOMACH: It's not that. You know that feeling I get sometimes?

STEWART: The puke feeling?

STOMACH: No. The gut feeling. The one where I know something even before Brain does?

STEWART: Yeah.

STOMACH: I'm having it right now.

STEWART: About what?

STOMACH: Freddy.

Another ten minutes went by.
Still no Freddy.

BRAIN: I know why Stomach had that gut feeling. When he said 'I'm back!'—

STEWART: I know, I know.

BRAIN: —he meant he was back in the bully business.

STEWART: I said, I know.

BRAIN: And we were his first victim.

STEWART: I KNOW!

BRAIN: His new kind of bullying, now that he lost some weight, is to trick people and outsmart them instead of beating them up. Like getting us to just hand him all our money like that.

STOMACH: I had a feeling—

STEWART: Can you guys shut up please?

STOMACH: —a gut feeling.

The bell sounded, ending sixth period.

Stewart, with his head down, slouched off to science class. Along the way he took stock of things:

The baseball, signed by none other than More Berg
(who ever that was) was still in Cunningham's
backpack.
Big Pops was likely going to kill him because of this.
In two days, he had lost $1,350.
He was exhausted.
He was starving.

It was hard to imagine the day getting any worse, and yet that is exactly what it did.

When he walked into science class, his teacher handed him a note from the principal.

It read:

Report to my office immediately after 8th period to
discuss your unreported absence on Tuesday and to
take a truancy report home to your ~~parent~~ guardian.

Perfect.

Not only was he in trouble for missing classes Tuesday, but he would have to explain everything to Big Pops. Then his grandfather would find out he didn't have the baseball.

Stewart figured he'd never see Friday morning still alive.

He spent all of science class ignoring the teacher and having crazy thoughts. When Spanish class started, those crazy thoughts started seeming a little less crazy and more just weird. By the end of class, those thoughts had become down right rational. In fact, they were his only choice.

The bell rang, ending 8th period. He shuffled with the herd out into the hall. Everyone headed to the right, toward the main entrance of the building. That was the direction Stewart should have gone as well in order to report to the principal's office.

He went left instead.

Toward the library.

To hide.

All night.

It seemed his only shot at survival.

Stewart slipped into the library and zipped around a tall magazine rack, crouching down to hide.

He heard the librarian across the room at his desk, packing up for the day. Stewart remained still. The librarian turned off the lights and Stewart heard him lock the door behind him as he left.

Stewart dug a little flashlight out of his backpack. Then he crept quietly though the maze of bookshelves toward the back of the room, looking for for section 919.6. (Of course Stewart had the entire Dewey Decimal System committed to memory.)

He plunked his backpack down and went back to he front of the library to plunder supplies. In no time, he had a nice little set-up with a reading chair and a desk lamp.

He pulled a book out of section 919.6, opened to a random page and settled in to read.

Not long after that, Stewart began to formulate a new plan.

The rest of his body didn't like the sound of it at all.

BRAIN: Oh, come on …

STEWART: This will work.

BRAIN: We need paint.

STEWART: Yep.

BRAIN: Where are we going to get paint?

STEWART: Where do you think?

BRAIN: I asked you.

STEWART: Look around.

BRAIN: Not my job to look around.

EYES: We're in the library.

BRAIN: We're in the library.

STEWART: Where else are we?

BRAIN: Huh?

STEWART: Think!

BRAIN: I'M TOO TIRED TO THINK!

STEWART: We're at school. We're alone at school.

STOMACH: I'm so hungry!

STEWART: What did I just say?!

STOMACH: We're at school?

STEWART: We'll just stroll down to the cafeteria.

STOMACH: Yes! Please hurry.

STEWART: Have a nice meal, then head over to the art room for some paint.

BRAIN: Oh, yeah. I should have thought of that.

STEWART: Yes, you should have.

BRAIN: But what about the grass?

STEWART: Science lab.

BRAIN: The spear?

STEWART: Theater Department.

BRAIN: So you've thought of everything?

STEWART: I think so.

BRAIN: Good. So you don't need me for this. Gladly sit this plan out.

STEWART: Oh, I need you brain. More than ever. To pull this off, I need you thinking every step of the way. And legs, I need you ready and able to run like the wind. Eyes, you'll need to be ever vigilant. Stomach, you have to be brave. Lungs, get ready for a work-out. For us to pull this off, we have to work together like we never have before. I know we can do it! Everybody with me?!

BRAIN, STOMACH, EYES, LUNGS, LEGS: YES!!!

BLADDER: I have to pee.

As usual, a river of students flowed from the buses at the curb to the front door of West Plain High, their minds on the school day ahead, the tests they were about to take or the homework they forgot to do, the girls they liked and the boys that they wanted to sit with at lunch.

But not as usual, they were all being watched by a Micronesian warrior peering down on them from the rooftop. He knelt behind the short wall at the edge of the roof, spying on the students below, prepared to carry forth his mission with honor. Dressed in traditional warrior attire, tribal tattoos adorning his body, spear held firmly by his side, a noble Micronesian, proud and strong.

Well, it was really just Stewart dressed up in a grass skirt with paint all over his body.

As the day began inside the school, Stewart knew the cafeteria staff would find the remnants of his midnight meal, the art teacher would find some open cans of black paint, the drama teacher might notice a fake spear missing from the props room, the science teacher would see someone had cut down all the tall grass in the ecosystem aquarium and the librarian would find a stack of books left on the floor in front of section 919.6 with titles like 'Micronesian Culture and History.'

Stewart modeled himself after a picture of a warrior found on page 114 of *Tribes of the Micronesian Islands*.

After his outfit was complete, he spent the rest of the night reading the table. His plan was built on speed, surprise and good old capitalism. He would have to know how to get around quickly if he was to end the day with the money that was stolen from him and Big Pops' baseball. So he memorized the layout of the school, found classrooms he had never seen, halls he'd never been down, found good places to hide and mapped his eventual getaway. Then he visited the administration office and found the file of first biggest bully at West Plain High.

With a map of the school and Freddy's class schedule committed to his memory, he slept for a few restless hours in the library, rose with the sun and made his way to the roof.

After the last kids entered the school below him, Stewart turned and jogged toward the maintenance access stairs to the roof.

That's when he hit snafu #1.

His feet got tangled in the spear, causing him to trip. He scrambled to catch his footing, and instead, stepped onto the shaft of the spear as he struggled to get it out of his way, snapping it in two as he lost his balance and feel to the ground.

Then, while trying to pick himself back up, he jammed the pointy end of half the spear into the roof, and pushed himself up. The spear dug into the asphalt then snapped again.

This was bad. The spear was important.

In addition to speed and surprise, his plan was built on terror. He intended to scare Freddy into giving his money back. Then, he planned to use all of that money to simply buy his grandfather's ball back from Cunningham.

Stewart looked down at his mostly naked, plumpish, painted body.

With the spear by his side, he was a passably scary Micronesian warrior. Without the spear, he was a geek dressed for halloween a few months too early.

This would not do.

He had to get a another spear.

Luckily, he knew a quick route to the theater prop room through the kitchen behind the cafeteria and across the stage. He could grab a spear and be ready to accost Freddy.

He ran down the steps to the first floor landing. The maintenance access stairs were accessible from a seldom used hallway on the west side of the school. He sprinted down this hall and ducked through the staff entrance of the cafeteria kitchen.

He saw a light on in the kitchen freezer and correctly guessed the cook was pulling food out to prepare for lunch.

Stewart weaved his way past the freezer and the cook inside, then out the far exit.

First period had started, so no one should be in the hall. He knew kids with free period would be making their way toward the music arts wing to gamble, but he wasn't near that hall.

All he had to do was sprint fifty yards left down the hall to the rear entrance of the auditorium, then through the dark stage to the prop room on the far side.

Ten yards down the hall he hit snafu #2.

Stewart took three quarters of a second to calculate how much larger snafu #2 was compared to snafu #1.

He came up with 398% larger, which was a lot. He took a third of a second to double check his math.

Yep. Snafu #2 was 398% larger than Snafu #1.

Snafu #2 was Big Pops.

Stewart heard his grandfather's voice in the main hall, around the corner from his current position.

"Stewart?" Big Pops was calling. "Where are you, Stewart?"

What was he doing here?

"We have a meeting, Stewart."

A meeting? What did he mean?

Just then, Stewart's brain chimed in with some urgent information:

BRAIN: Based on Big Pops' estimated position around the corner, we can safely assume he cannot see us.

However, the increased volume in his voice indicates he is traveling towards our location.

STEWART: Could you calculate his speed and an estimated time until he can visually identify us?

BRAIN: Of course I could. But I'm not gonna.

STEWART: Why not?

BRAIN: We don't have time.

STEWART: It's a fairly simple calculation. Shouldn't take you more than a fraction of a second to—

BRAIN: GET MOVING!

STEWART: Oh. Right.

Stewart started sprinting again, flinging himself through the door to the auditorium. He carefully peered through the small window in the door and saw Big Pops round the corner.

"Stewart? Where are you? We got to go to a meeting."

His grandfather looked down the the hallway, then turned back the way he came.

He must not have seen his grandson running down the hall in nothing but a grass skirt and glasses.

Phew.

What did Big Pops mean, 'we got to go to a meeting'? It sounded like the kind of thing the killer says to his unsuspecting victim in one of those PG-13 movies.

That must be it.

Big Pops was there to kill Stewart.

BRAIN: You think?

STEWART: He spent time in prison, you know.

His brain didn't sound convinced, but Stewart didn't have time to argue. He had to grab a spear and get on with his plan, regardless of the fact that Big Pops was now roaming the halls of the school looking for him.

He ran across the stage to the props room on the far side. As he did, he was vaguely aware of a few things that were different than when he visited the auditorium in the middle of the night.

One was that the lights were on. In the night he used his flashlight to find his way around. The auditorium was particularly dark. But now, stage lights were shining down on Stewart as he ran across the stage.

And all the lights were on over the seats as well. Stewart noticed just how big the auditorium looked from the stage with the whole room lit, a view he had never had before.

Another difference was that kids were sitting in the front row seats.

This difference didn't register with Stewart until he was halfway across the stage.

Too late to turn around.

Too late to do anything but keep running.

The kids in the front row were having a Public Speaking class. They saw a plump Micronesian warrior sprint across the stage wearing nothing but a grass skirt and glasses.

The teacher had her back to the stage, and therefore saw nothing. She did notice the eyes of her students following something, and registering surprise, but by the time she turned her head, Stewart had reached the wings on the far side of the stage.

The students were so surprised at what they saw, they said nothing.

Until later, that is.

But Stewart didn't know that his nearly naked, tattoo covered body had shocked them into total silence. He assumed they would start screaming any second, so he kept on running, pushing his way through the curtains hanging in the wings to a side exit that took him into the science wing of West Plain High.

It wasn't until the door shut behind him that he realized he had forgotten all about grabbing a new new spear from the prop room. He couldn't turn around and risk an encounter with the Public Speaking teacher. He would have to continue unarmed.

Which would definitely make things tougher.

As would the fact that the principal was now roaming the halls.

"Mr. Pops?" the principal called from further down the science wing, his back to Stewart, who had pressed his flesh against the wall trying feebly to hide. "Mr. Big Pops? Where did you go?"

The principal turned down the main hall.

Stewart took one tenth of one second to organize the list of current snafus, first chronologically:

Broken spear
Big Pops looking for me
Spotted by Public Speaking Class
Principal looking for Big Pops.

Then in order of concern, smallest to largest:

Spotted by Public Speaking Class
Principal looking for Big Pops
Broken spear
Big Pops looking for me.

Stewart took seven tenths of a second to calculate his odds of successfully completing his plan given these new obstacles, and concluded that his chances were incredibly slim. But his chances were incredibly slim without these obstacles, just ever so slightly less so.

There was no sense giving up now, he reasoned. Might as well press on.

He had missed his opportunity to confront Freddy at his locker after first period. He would have to circle back to the biggest bully at West Plain High after dealing with the second biggest bully at West Plain High.

Stewart cut through a dark science lab, across a hall, into an unoccupied art studio, then out into the music arts wing, just four doors down from the xylophone practice room.

"Mr. Pops? Where are you?"

The principal appeared further down the hall, heading toward Stewart.

So back he went, through the unused art studio, out into the hall...

"Stewart?! Where are you?"

Big Pops was walking away from Stewart toward the main hall of West Plain High.

Stewart dashed across the hall, into the dark science lab and back out into the hall ...

"I told you you we weren't crazy," he heard a girl's voice say.

The entire Public Speaking Class was standing in the hall with their teacher, pointing at Stewart as he emerged from the lab.

The teacher considered the plump, tattooed kid wearing noting but a grass skirt and glasses that stood in front of her.

"Oh my," was all she could say.

Stewart stepped carefully backwards toward the science lab with his slow and deliberate steps, trying to suggest to the teacher and kids in front of him that everything was normal, everything was fine, really, no need to be shocked by what you are seeing.

He gave up that effort when a tall public speaker screamed, "Get him!"

The pack of students lurched forward, leaving the stunned teacher behind. Stewart turned and ran.

Through the dark science lab.

"Stewart?" He heard, but didn't see Big Pops.

Through the unused art studio.

Glancing over his shoulder he saw the pack of Public Speakers still chasing him.

Back into the music wing.

He ran right past the xylophone practice room and across the intersection with the main hall.

Glancing to the right, he saw the principal walking back toward the front of the school, still looking for Big Pops.

"Hey, you!" Stewart shouted as he ran past, which bothered his brain immensely.

BRAIN: What did you do that for?! Now he's gonna see us!

STEWART: Calculate our running speed, the width of the main hall and the time for the principal to hear and respond to my shouts. Then, calculate the location of the pack of kids following us while plotting a line of sight vector at that moment for the principal and get back to me.

BRAIN: Ah. He will see *them*.

STEWART: Exactly.

BRAIN: But how does that help us?

STEWART: You'll see.

"Hey, you kids," the principal called, when he saw the pack of Public Speakers running across the hall. "Why aren't you in class?" And he set off after them.

Stewart made a sharp right turn at the end of the hall, then another right turn down the history wing.

He ran past history classes, in which a teacher might well be talking about tribal warriors of the Pacific Islands. Little did they know, there was a living model sprinting past their class at that very moment.

When he reached the main hall, he turned left and ran as fast as he could. He needed a little distance between him and the Public Speakers.

The he made another left down a short narrow hall, passing doors to maintenance closets.

BRAIN: Warning! Warning! This is a dead end hall! Warning! Warning!

Of course his brain was right. This hall was a dead end.

There was, however, a steel door at the end, but it wasn't a door you should ever go through. It was a fire exit, a steel door with a red sign explaining that opening this door would set of an alarm, summon the fire department and should never, ever be used except in the case of an emergency.

A second sign reiterated this point, explaining that using this door for something other than an emergency would certainly get you in a lot of trouble with the school and with the cops who would also be summoned.

A third sign simply said 'Don't even think about it.'

Stewart headed right for the door.

BRAIN: Warning! Warning!

While reading the table the night before, Stewart learned more than just the layout of the school. He learned about the condition of it.

He saw broken sinks and water fountains that wouldn't turn on. There were computer keyboards missing keys and chalk boards that were cracked. Some doors were hard to open, others wouldn't stay closed. Chairs and desks wobbled on bent legs.

Stewart never noticed the poor condition of West Plain High, probably because he was too busy being nervous about starting a new school. But he could see clearly that a lot of things were broken around this place.

In poker, when you are counting on a good card to show up, you call your hand 'a draw.' If you know how likely the odds are that the card you need will in fact show up, you might bet on your hand to win.

And that's exactly what Stewart did by running right at the fire door.

The pack of Public Speakers, carried by their momentum, plowed into the wall at the end of the hall, being careful not to open the fire door for fear of setting off the alarms and being hauled off to jail.

Then they all looked around for Stewart.

Then, the principal plowed into the Public Speakers.

Stewart realized why grass skirts never caught on outside of tropical areas. Even though the sun was out and it was fairly mild by West Plain standards, he was chilly standing outside in his.

The alarm on the door was broken. Stewart had won his bet.

Stewart waited until he guessed that the principal hauled the public speakers off to his office for an explanation for roaming the halls during classes, then yanked on the door he had just passed through.

It didn't budge.

Stewart added one item to the bottom of his chronological list of snafus and that same item to the top of the list in order of concern:

Locked out of West Plain High.

While the alarm on the fire door was broken, the door itself was not. Being an emergency exit, it only opened out. He sure couldn't walk in the front door, past the administrative office in the foyer looking like he did.

His plan to terrify and shock the first and second biggest bullies at West Plain High with his Micronesian warrior outfit and his sharp and dangerous-looking spear was utterly ruined.

The money was gone.

The baseball was gone.

Stewart gave up.

He had no choice.

He would have to run away.

BRAIN: Run away?

LEGS: We just ran away.

STEWART: I mean, run away from home.

BRAIN: Home?

STEWART: Our new home. Big Pops' house.

BRAIN: Are you crazy?

LEGS: We're exhausted.

STEWART: We don't have a choice. Big Pops wants to kill me. We can't get the baseball back. We have to run away.

STOMACH: Can we get some breakfast on the way? I'm hungry.

STEWART: You just ate.

STOMACH: A midnight snack is not a meal. I want pork roll.

STEWART: We can't get pork roll.

STOMACH: We're a growing kid. I'm starving again!

STEWART: We don't have any money.

BRAIN: Forget money. We don't have any clothes.

STEWART: I didn't say it was gonna be easy. I said we didn't have a choice.

And so over the objections of every part of his body, Stewart set out to run away. He headed for the road in front of West Plain High, walking along the side of the school, crouching low under the classroom windows.

As he turned around the corner to the front of the school he ran into Big Pops.

Literally.

His head plowed right into Big Pop's chest and his arms flailed around the grown up. The two were a tangled mess of grandfather and grandson.

"I was looking for you," Big Pops said sharply as Stewart tried to unravel himself.

"Here I am," Stewart said, heart racing, eyes wide.

Big Pops pushed Stewart back and looked over his outfit.

"What are you wearing?"

"Oh, nothing," Stewart shrugged.

"I see that. How come?"

"It's a project, class project about this and that—"

"I got a call from the principal," Big Pops cut him off. "Something about you missing classes Tuesday."

"Oh, that," Stewart said, trying his best to sound casual. "That was some kind of mix up with the attendance sheet and some other things that got all confused."

"Oh yeah?"

"Oh yeah," Stewart confirmed, nodding his head confidently.

"That's not what he said," Big Pops said.

"Who?"

"The principal."

"Oh, well, that's because—" Stewart started.

"And you didn't come home last night."

"Sure I did," Stewart said, bluffing. "You just didn't notice."

"And he said you weren't in class this morning."

"Who?"

"The principal."

"Why wouldn't I be in class?"

"That's what I said," Big Pops said. "So I went looking for you."

"Why are you looking out here?" Stewart asked.

"Because you weren't in there," Big Pops answered.

"Why were you looking for me in there?"

"You weren't home. Where else you gonna be?" Big Pops asked. "Anyway, come on, we got a meeting."

Yep.

A meeting.

Big Pops wanted a meeting because Stewart lost his baseball. He wanted to get Stewart here, where he least expected it. He wanted to get Stewart like he'd probably got other guys before, and for which he had been thrown in jail.

"Let's go," Big Pops said, motioning behind him.

This is it.

Stewart's vision was clouded by water filling his eyes. His lungs filled with air, getting ready to sob.

He got ready for the end.

But just then his ever-working, always nimble, super efficient brain, came to a conclusion that somehow had eluded Stewart since Wednesday night.

BRAIN: Dude, Big Pops isn't gonna kill you. He's your *grandfather*.

What his brain told him was so utterly and obviously true that relief spread through his tired and hungry body in a flash, leaving him instantly comforted and somehow even more exhausted.

He was no longer afraid, but the tears came anyway.

Stewart rushed forward to tangle himself up with Big Pops again, hugging him hard, trying to explain everything to him in one burst.

This is what it sounded like:

STEWART: Big Pops, ball ... bus ... loaded dice ... bully took ... Moe ... can't ... plan ... hungry ...

"Whaaale," Big Pops said quietly, patting Stewart's naked back. "If you don't take any wooden nickels you sure won't get the dimes."

Stewart and Big Pops sat down, backs against the side of the school and Stewart told him everything. Clearly this time.

Big Pops listened, not saying a word, nodding his head now and then when something suddenly made sense to him. Like why he wanted to learn to play craps. And when Stewart explained why he came home late, or not at all.

When Stewart got to the end of it all, Big Pops spoke.

"I'm awfully sorry that baseball caused you so much trouble," he said. "You know, that ball really doesn't matter that much to me, it's just—"

"It does to me," Stewart said, cutting him off.

Stewart was glad his brain was right and Big Pops wasn't planning on killing him. He was also relieved that Big Pops wasn't mad about the baseball. But Stewart realized that even though he didn't know who Moe Berg was, or really, even cared, he hadn't been trying to get it back from the second biggest bully at West Plain High just for Big Pops. He was trying for himself too.

This was his new school.

He didn't want to be the geek that could get pushed around here. He had enough to deal with just getting used to living with Big Pops. He didn't need that too.

"So you want to get it back?" Big Pops asked him.

Stewart nodded.

"Might as well get the money back too then," Big Pops said.

Stewart nodded again.

"We're gonna need a new plan."

It took Big Pops just thirty-two seconds of quiet thought before he started laying out a new and improved plan. It was clear to Stewart that Big Pops had planned things like this before. He dissected Stewart's original plan, threw away the parts he didn't like, kept the parts he did, and added a whole new dimension to it.

Within ten minutes, he had the new plan carefully explained to Stewart and they were on their way to the principal's office.

Stewart thought maybe he should have wiped off his painted on tattoos and maybe even put some clothes on for a meeting with the principal, but Big Pops said absolutely not.

"That get-up of yours is perfect," he told him. "Gonna work great. Big part of the new plan."

"But I broke the spear."

"Bah," Big Pops said. "Who would be afraid of a fake spear anyway?"

The principal was in the middle of explaining to the public speakers that it was absolutely impossible that they saw a tribal warrior from Micronesia running through the halls of the school wearing nothing but a grass skirt and glasses when Big Pops and Stewart barged into his office.

Being unable to explain away the obvious contradiction presented by the sudden appearance of a Micronesian warrior wearing nothing but a grass skirt and glasses, the principal simply dismissed the public speakers and offered Big Pops and Stewart a seat in front of his desk.

"If a tree drops an acorn," the principal started, looking alternately at Stewart and Big Pops. "Where does it fall?"

Stewart looked at Big Pops. Big Pops looked at Stewart. Neither one knew who was supposed to answer.

After a few moments of uncomfortable silence, Stewart took a shot at it.

"On the ground?"

"Yes," The principal allowed. "But *where* on the ground?"

"On *top* of the ground?" Stewart tried.

"Where in relation to the tree?"

"Where is the ground in relation to the tree?"

"What I am getting at is," the principal said. "We want to make sure the tree is fertilizing the acorn."

"What kind of fertilizer?" Big Pops asked.

"Good question," the principal said. "One that I could ask you, Mr. Big Pops. What kind of fertilizer indeed?"

"Oh, I see," Big Pops said. Stewart was relieved to hear that. "You are wondering, because of Stewart's recent and somewhat unexplained absences, if his acorn fell near or far from me, the tree—"

"Yes!" the principal exclaimed.

"—and furthermore, if me, the tree, is watching over Stewart, the acorn—"

"Precisely!" His bushy mustache stretched over a wide smile.

"—which is all well and good except for a couple of things here," Big Pops said, leaning forward and lowering his voice. "I'm not the tree. I'm the tree's tree. And I have to say, the tree's tree is a little concerned about *your* fertilizer."

"My fertilizer?"

"Here at the school."

"Whatever do you mean?" The principal asked.

"I mean there are some things going on here that don't strike me as fertilizing."

"I must insist—" the principal started, struggling to maintain his smile.

"Listen for a second Mr. Principal," Big Pops said, still talking softly. "Mind if I call you Prince?" Big Pops continued without an answer. "Listen, Prince, I know about the craps game."

"Craps game?" the principal answered, trying to look shocked. But Stewart could tell he was bluffing.

"Yep, the craps game" Big Pops said plainly. "What's your cut?"

"My cut?" the principal said

"Ten percent? Twenty?" Big Pops asked. "I'm guessing twenty."

The principal tried a few more bluffs.

First he pretended not to understand what craps was.

Then he pretended to be offended at the suggestion that there was a craps game going on at West Plain High.

Then he pretended to be shocked that Big Pops would suggest that he, the principal of the school, was making money from the game by taking twenty percent of Cunningham's winnings.

But it didn't work.

Big Pops knew the principal was in on the craps game. He figured that out as soon as Stewart told him about Monday morning. That was why he let Cunningham go while punishing Stewart. He didn't want to break up the craps game.

"So Prince, Stewart and me—" Big Pops started.

"Stewart and *I*," Stewart corrected.

"Stewart and I," Big Pops said. "Are not here to judge. We're here for something else. And we can keep a secret just fine. You see where I'm going with this?"

The principal nodded his head slowly. Big Pops went on to tell him to stay out of the music wing all day, no matter what he heard was happening down there. For that, he wouldn't report to the Board of Education that the principal was allowing and participating in gambling in the school.

The principal's bushy mustache bunched up over his clenched mouth and started twitching. He realized he had no choice, and nodded his head, agreeing to Big Pops' demands.

With that done, Big Pops and Stewart headed for the door.

"Excuse me," the principal said, mustache still twitching. "But what are you here for?"

"What's that Prince?" Big Pops asked.

"You said you were here for something else. What might that be, may I ask?"

"Whaaale," Big Pops said walking out the door. "You can't ask stupid questions, but you sure can get a stupid answer."

From his explorations the night before, Stewart knew exactly how to get to the school's basement without being seen. And once they got there, he knew exactly where to find the electrical panel.

The electrical panel was a big metal box that contained circuit breakers. Each circuit breaker controlled the electricity for different areas of the school. You could turn the power off for say, science lab #1 by turning off the circuit breaker labeled 'Science Lab #1.' Once the power was off, the lights in that room would turn off.

Of course you could do the same thing for any other room in the school. Like the xylophone practice room.

Big Pops took his position in front of the electrical box and Stewart headed back the way they came. He was full of confidence in his grass skirt and his painted tattoos. As he made his way unseen through the school, sneaking past classrooms and through empty labs, he had no doubt this plan would work.

He would stand outside of the xylophone practice room, listening to the craps game, waiting. When Big Pops turned off the breaker, killing the lights, he would open the door quietly, sneak into the circle of players, strike a terrifying pose and wait.

Stewart ducked into the gym while imagining the terror the players and Cunningham would feel when the lights were suddenly turned on and they saw that a Micronesian tribal warrior had materialized in the middle of their dice game! They would think Stewart was a spirit coming to haunt them. Fear would grip their minds. They would all be completely freaked and run straight for the door.

Stewart crawled behind the bleachers, hiding himself from the gym class playing basketball on the opposite side of the gym as he pictured himself in the xylophone practice room, left alone to calmly collect the baseball, signed by none other than Moe Berg, from Cunningham's backpack and he would move on to the second part of the plan.

Big Pops was right. This was much better than shaking a wooden spear at them.

This had special effects and surprise.

It was a great plan.

BRAIN: Excuse me ...
STEWART: What?
BRAIN: I hate to be a nag.
STEWART: Then don't be.
BRAIN: It's just that this plan—
STEWART: This is a great plan.
BRAIN: Well, I thought so too, but—
STEWART: It is.
BRAIN: It's just that I think we forgot something.
STEWART: This. Is. A. Great. Plan.
BRAIN: Right, but how will Big Pops know when to turn off the lights?

He froze.

How would Big Pops know when to turn the lights off?

They never talked about that.

Oh boy.

Stewart calculated the amount of time it took him to get to his current position behind the gym bleachers and added that to the amount of time it would take to get from the gym bleachers to the xylophone practice room. Then he used several methods to estimate the time Big Pops would think it would take for him to reach the xylophone practice room from the basement and subtracted one time from the other.

After a full two seconds during which he came up with 37 different answers, he realized it was pointless. There were too many variables. Big Pops didn't even know where the xylophone practice room was.

All he could conclude was that he should get there as soon as possible.

He started scurrying on his hands and knees as fast as he could. He went so fast his knees burned on the hard gym floor. By the time he emerged from the bleachers they were bleeding. He snuck out the far door to the gym when the class was shooting at the basket on the opposite end.

Stewart threw caution to the wind, sprinting down the center of the music wing hall, knees bleeding, bare feet slapping loudly on the tile floor, grass skirt parting dangerously in the breeze he created.

Halfway to the xylophone practice room, he saw that he was too late.

The light pouring out from under the door into the hallway abruptly disappeared.

He ran faster, hoping he could get to the door and inside the room before Big Pops turned the breaker back on. But he knew Big Pops would only leave the power off for 15 seconds. As he arrived at the door, light spilled out from under it again.

Stewart heard voices inside the xylophone practice room.

"That was weird."

"We get a do-over."

"That roll doesn't count."

"What happened?"

Then Stewart heard Cunningham grunt, dice were rolled and the craps game started up again.

Stewart bent over and struggled to catch his breath. He was winded and disappointed. But then, suddenly, he had another chance.

The lights went out again.

It took him less than a quarter of a second to understand that Big Pops must have realized the flaw in their plan as well. He must have been hoping Stewart could still salvage things.

And salvage things he did.

Or rather, salvage things he tried.

Stewart opened the door and stepped into the darkness.

But the darkness didn't last.

The lights came back on.

All the craps players in the circle turned to stare at the mostly naked kid with paint on his body, blood on his knees and a grass skirt around his waist as he pulled the door shut behind him. Cunningham, at the head of the circle pointed at Stewart and laughed. Then the other students started laughing too.

So much for striking terror into the heart of the second biggest bully at West Plain High.

Then the lights went out again.

Stewart reasoned correctly that Big Pops was freaking out down in the basement. Once he, like Stewart realized they hadn't thought out the whole timing thing, he didn't know what to do, so he was improvising.

Before Stewart could do anything, the lights came back on.

Then went out again.

The interval between the power going off and back on again was unpredictable but generally getting shorter. This was part of Big Pops' improvising.

The lights went out again.

"What's going on?" someone asked.

Guided by the memory of the now shattered plan, Stewart found himself making his way to the center of the room, directly in the middle of the dice game.

"Watch the money!" someone else screamed.

"Where's the dice?"

"I got a lot of cash riding on that roll!"

"Everybody freeze," Cunningham commanded in his low and slow voice. "The lights will come back on in a second."

The shouts of the players gave Stewart an idea. He kneeled down and in the darkness swept his arms out, scooping up all the cash laid out on the floor.

When the lights came back on all the kids in the room saw that the chunky kid in the grass skirt and glasses had a pile of their money bunched up in his fists.

They were no longer laughing at him. Instead they were scowling.

Stewart knew he had to act fast before Big Pops turned the lights out again.

He turned away from Cunningham, straightened up his short back, struggling to look like the confident and proud Micronesian warrior on page 114 of *Tribes of the Micronesia Islands*, then he threw the pile of money toward the far wall.

The lights went out again.

Everyone was silent in the darkness.

The lights came back on and the quiet lasted another two seconds more.

Then the room erupted as the players scrambled away from Stewart, pushing, shoving and shouting their way to the cash.

So far so good. The players were out of his way. The only thing left for him to deal with was the second biggest bully at West Plain High.

Stewart turned to face Cunningham, still struggling to look strong and warrior-like.

Cunningham regarded the funny-looking kid in the middle of the room. The bully grinned and cracked his knuckles.

The lights went out, then back on, then out again.

STOMACH: Hey guys, something's going on with me,
STEWART: This is not the time to puke.
STOMACH: No, it's nothing like that. In fact, it's the exact opposite.
STEWART: What do you mean?
STOMACH: I'm feeling good. I'm feeling strong.

Stewart tried to contact his brain to find out what his stomach was talking about, but his brain didn't respond. It couldn't stop itself from spinning around and around in Stewart's head making itself dizzy, but not in an unpleasant way.

Stewart took three quarters of a second to analyze these feelings and this caused him to remember something. Many somethings actually.

Feeling dizzy made him remember listening to his science teacher on Wednesday.

Remembering listening to his science teacher on Wednesday made him remember passing out.

Remembering passing out made him remember getting poked in the stomach with a tongue depressor by the nurse.

Remembering getting poked in the stomach with a tongue depressor by the nurse made him remember the feeling he had in the nurse's office.

Remembering that feeling he had in the nurses office made him remember how badly he wanted to have the feeling he had in the nurse's office again.

And then, suddenly he was having that feeling again.

The lights came back on.

Cunningham was staring at him, eyes squinted, mouth curled in a snarl. The second biggest bully at West Plain High was clearly not happy with the way the Micronesian Warrior had interrupted his craps game.

The lights went off again.

In the darkness, Stewart lavished in the feeling of connectedness that washed over him.

I am connected to the dark, he thought.

And to Big Pops turning the lights off and on.

And to the grass I can feel against my legs.

And to the field the grass came from.

The lights went back on.

Cunningham was closer to him now. Stewart noticed the snarl had turned into a smile, so he smiled back.

I am connected to Cunningham, he thought.

Then Cunningham punched him.

Cunningham's fist was so large it hit Stewart's left cheek, mouth and nose. Two out of three of these areas started bleeding immediately while the third instantly swelled up.

It was a hard punch and it hurt a lot. Somewhere in the back of his mind Stewart took a tenth of a second to rank the pain he was feeling as the third most physical pain he had felt in his life to date, but somehow, Stewart didn't fall over.

Because of the feeling.

NOSE: OW! Wow, that hurts!

MOUTH: Did I lose a tooth?

STEWART: I am connected to the dice on the floor—

MOUTH: I think I lost a tooth.

CHEEK: Do I look fat? I feel fat.

STEWART: —and to the xylophone practice room—

NOSE: I'm bleeding over here!

MOUTH: Me too!

CHEEK: I'm blowing up like a blimp.

STEWART: —and to the taste of blood—

MOUTH: That's my blood you are tasting.

NOSE: And mine.

STEWART: —and to the sound of the kids fighting for money—

MOUTH: What are you babbling about?

NOSE: Are you listening to us?

CHEEK: We're hurt!

BRAIN: SHUT UP! All of you. Quiet. It doesn't matter. You're hurt. So what? It doesn't matter. Got it? It doesn't matter.

They got it.

The blood didn't matter.

I am connected to the blood.

The pain didn't matter.

I am connected to the pain.

The lights went out again.

I am connected to my mom!

I am connected to my dad!

The lights came back on.

Cunningham pulled his fist pulled back to punch Stewart again, but before he could, the lights went out.

Stewart took one step, two feet to the left.

When the lights came back on, Cunningham swung, missing Stewart by two feet to the right. He lost his balance and staggered forward.

Stewart pulled his own right hand back, took aim at the side of Cunningham's huge head as he stumbled past him, closed his eyes and punched.

I am connected to my mom and dad who are dead.

Stewart's fist found Cunningham's temple.

The second biggest bully at West Plain High's momentum carried him forward, his eyes closing from the knock-out punch. Cunningham's arms flailed at his sides. He was like a tall tree, branches flapping as it falls in the woods, knocking over the other kids like saplings.

The xylophone practice room became completely silent.

The students on the ground watched as Stewart, the Micronesian Warrior, body covered with tribal tattoos stepped over Cunningham's thick legs, opened the bully's backpack and pulled from it a baseball.

A baseball signed by none other than Moe Berg.

The second part of Big Pops and Stewart's plan dealt with recovering the money from Freddy, the first biggest bully at West Plain High. It was complicated, calling for Big Pops to pose as a movie producer who wanted to make a film about Freddy's incredible weight loss and his impending comeback to the bullying trade.

It was an elaborate plan that would take days to complete. Stewart abandoned it, choosing a simpler strategy. Having Freddy's class schedule memorized he headed straight for the math wing.

He was still swimming in the feeling, still oblivious to his pain.

When he found the right geometry classroom, Stewart simply opened the door and walked in.

The whole class turned toward the interruption and saw Stewart, his nose and mouth dripping blood down the front of his face, glasses cocked to the side, knees bloody, the painted tattoos smearing, his grass skirt frayed and torn. The teacher started to say something, but thought better of it.

Stewart walked straight to Freddy and stood in front of his desk.

Freddy's jaw dropped and his eyes opened wide. Like the rest of the class, he couldn't understand what he was seeing.

Stewart raised his hand sharply and Freddy flinched. Stewart slammed the baseball down hard on the desk with a crack. He stared silently at Freddy.

Freddy nodded, reached into his pocket and laid the pile of money on the desk next to the baseball.

Stewart picked up the money and the baseball, turned and ran from the room because he knew he was going to cry and he didn't want to spoil his image as a proud, Micronesian warrior.

Turning down the hall running to the front of the school he ran once again right into Big Pops, and once again got tangled up in his grandfather. But this time, he didn't try to free himself.

Instead, he leaned into Big Pops and tears poured out of his closed eyes.

The rest of the day was a blur for Stewart, which of course, is highly unusual. Stewart could vividly remember what socks he wore to his fifth grade graduation. He could recite his lines as the Slice of Cheese from his second grade play about nutrition. He could take you to the spot in the woods behind his old house where he found a rock shaped like an eagle's head.

He usually remembered everything.

But he didn't remember much about the car ride home. Or how at home, Big Pops helped him clean up his wounds and wash off his tattoos. About them ordering and eating two whole pizzas. He didn't remember his grandfather tucking him into bed for the first time since he moved in with him.

But he did remember waking up in the middle of the night.

He saw someone sitting in a chair in middle of his room. That person had a small flash light in one hand, shining down on a notebook on his lap. With the other hand, he was writing and writing.

Stewart was still half asleep and wasn't sure where he was. He blinked his eyes, trying to see who it was on the chair.

"Mom?" he asked.

"No," a man's voice answered.

"Dad?"

"Your mom and dad are gone," Big Pops said, putting his pen down. "Remember?"

And of course, Stewart did.

"Big Pops," Stewart said. "Why did Mom and Dad go to Micronesia?"

"There was a typhoon," Big Pops answered. "They went to see if they could help out. They told you that before they went, didn't they?"

"Yeah," Stewart said. "They did."

"I think your parents were very brave, going half way around the world to help some people out."

"Why were they riding bikes?" Stewart asked.

"It sounds like they had to," Big Pops said. "Sounds like there wasn't much gas. They were saving it for the trucks moving stuff around."

"Like the truck that hit them?"

"Yes."

"Why was the truck going so fast?"

"Sounds like they had medical supplies—"

"Band-Aids?" Stewart interrupted.

"Yep," Big Pops answered. "And food."

"Rice?"

"Yep. Didn't I tell you this already?"

"Yep," Stewart answered. "Where were Mom and Dad going?"

"To help unload the truck when it got to the folks that needed help."

"Why did the truck have to hit Mom and Dad?"

"I don't suppose it had to. But it did," Big Pops said quietly. "Sometimes things don't go the way they are planned."

Big Pops turned off his flashlight.

"Stewart," he said. "Do you mind if I sit here a while more?"

"No."

"Hey Stewart."

"Yes?"

"I think you are very brave too," Big Pops told him.

Stewart thought about that for one third of a second and realized his grandfather was right. He was brave. Just like his parents.

"Why don't you go back to sleep?" Big Pops asked.

For the first time in many nights, his stomach wasn't screaming at him that it was hungry. and he wasn't worried that his grandfather was going to kill him. And his body felt a little less sore. So he did.

Oddly, he dreamed of neon-colored spider webs.

The first thing Stewart saw when he woke up was the empty chair in the middle of the room. He jumped out of bed and grabbed the notebook Big Pops left sitting on the chair to see what his grandfather had been writing. He was surprised to see page after page of the same two words.

'Moe Berg.'

He noticed right away that the name was never written in Big Pop's usual hard to read blend of block letters and cursive. Instead, it was written again and again and again in a manner that was similar to, but not exactly like, the way Moe Berg had signed Big Pops' baseball.

Suddenly, much became clear to Stewart.

Still in his pajamas he dashed out of his room, notebook in hand and found Big Pops sitting in his easy chair, TV tray in front of him, eating his morning pork roll and toast.

"Counterfeiter," Stewart said.

"Good morning to you too," Big Pops said.

"That's what you went to jail for," Stewart continued. "You were a counterfeiter."

"*Are* a counterfeiter," Big Pops corrected him. "I *are* a counterfeiter."

"Am," Stewart corrected him.

"I *am* a counterfeiter," Big Pops agreed. "It's not something you grow out of. It's a gift you carry with you always."

Stewart looked at the TV. Something was different.

All this week there had been no baseball sitting on top of the TV where there had been one baseball. But now there were three baseballs.

Stewart walked to the TV and looked at them closer. All three were signed by none other than Moe Berg.

Stewart looked back at Big Pops.

"Pretty good work, wouldn't you say?"

Stewart looked back at the baseballs, then back at Big Pops and nodded his head.

Then Big Pops made a confession.

"I didn't lend you the baseball just so you could be cool," he told Stewart. "I lent you the baseball so all the other kids at school would want to be cool too. Then I could sell them a baseball just like the one that was making you so cool."

This information was so baffling that it took Stewart an incredible five and one third seconds to process it and understand what it meant.

Big Pops was trying to sell counterfeit baseballs. And the only reason he was anxious for Stewart to bring the first baseball back was so he could copy the signature accurately.

From his experience this week, Stewart knew a thing or two about bad plans and this was clearly one. Here is a partial list of problems with Big Pops' plan to sell counterfeit baseballs to Students at West Plain High:

A Baseball signed by Moe Berg was not a video game, MP3 player or a cell phone, therefore it was unlikely to be perceived as cool by the kids at West Plain High.
No one at West Plain High knew who Moe Berg was.
No one at West Plain High cared who Moe Berg was.

Stewart shared this list with Big Pops who was downright shocked.

"Kids don't know who Moe Berg was?"

Stewart shook his head.

"Moe Berg was a major league baseball player," Big Pops told him. "And a spy. Can you imagine that? Played catcher, and spied on the enemy during World War II. Isn't that incredible?"

Stewart admitted that it was, but he still didn't think kids at West Plain High would care. Certainly not enough to want to buy a counterfeit baseball signed by none other than Big Pops. He told his grandfather this.

"Whaaale," Big Pops said. "Every dog has his day except when they learn old tricks."

This of course didn't make any sense. At least, at first.

Stewart looked at Big Pops, who was looking at the three baseballs on top of the TV.

"You gonna play online poker?" Stewart asked.

"I suppose," Big Pops said, but instead of pushing away his tray and picking up his laptop computer, he just kept staring at the baseballs.

Stewart took approximately one second to consider carefully what Big Pops had said.

STEWART: Every dog has his day ...
BRAIN: Why would he say that?
STEWART: I think he was talking about himself.
BRAIN: He's not a dog.
STEWART: I know, but still ...
BRAIN: What about the 'old tricks' part?

Stewart told his brain what he thought it meant and his brain agreed.

Big Pops wanted a job.

Stewart and Big Pops spent most of the day playing catch with one of the counterfeit baseballs. While they tossed the ball back and forth, they made one more plan.

Here is a summary:

Step 1: Monday morning, explain to the principal that Stewart and Big Pops would forget all about

> the illegal craps game that he allowed and partici-
> pated in, in exchange for hiring Big Pops as the
> school's maintenance man, a position that badly
> needed to be filled.
>
> Step 2: Big Pops would become the best maintenance
> man at West Plain High.
>
> Step 3: Even though the first and second biggest bul-
> lies at West Plain High knew the true identity of the
> mostly naked Micronesian Warrior seen running
> through the halls, Stewart would deny it was in fact
> him. Instead of capitalizing on the fame associated
> with the Micronesian Warrior's daring exploits,
> Stewart would instead quietly fit in with the stu-
> dents at his new school.
>
> Step 4: There would be no more online poker or talk of
> gambling on dice. Nor would Big Pops teach Stewart
> how to be a counterfeiter, even though Big Pops
> really wanted to. These were not appropriate activi-
> ties for a household with a kid of Stewart's age.
>
> Step 5: Once a month Big Pops and Stewart would
> visit the graves of Stewart's mom and dad.
>
> Step 6: Pork roll for breakfast only once a week.
>
> Step 7: Figure out what it meant to dream of neon-
> colored spider webs.

In the days and weeks and months ahead, Step 7 would prove to be the toughest part of the new plan. Stewart suspected the dream was related to the feeling he had twice (and never again) of being connected to a lot of things, but most importantly, to his parents, even though they were gone.

Furthermore, through long conversations with his brain, stomach and other body parts, conversations that sometimes lasted as much as two or three minutes, he theorized that the dream was in fact proof that the feeling was more than a feeling, that it was in fact, a fact. He knew that if he could ever have the feeling or the dream again, his mind, being what it was, which was amazingly sharp, he could prove this theory promptly and put the matter to rest.

But he never did.

So he never could.

Other than that, the plan went perfectly.

THE END

ACKNOWLEDGMENTS

I'm grateful to many for their help in the creation of *Neon-colored Spider Webs*. Celia Silver, Jonah Rubin and Ellie Dykstra were careful readers and offered valuable feedback on early drafts. Terry McGovern invited me into his classroom after reading the book with his students. The discussions there were encouraging, helpful and fun. Terry's feedback as an educator was integral and I appreciate his dedication to creative writing in the classroom. Donna and Allan Rubin lent their much-needed proofreading skills. Allan's help was also crucial to my research in the mathematics of student invisibility. Tony Bennett created the cover, and Peter Silver designed and set the interior. Huge thanks to all of these creative, talented and generous friends and most especially to my family.

Made in the USA
Lexington, KY
12 December 2011